Dolores

also by
BRUCE BROOKS

Dolores

seven stories about her

BRUCE BROOKS

HARPERCOLLINS*PUBLISHERS*

Library of Congress Cataloging-in-Publication Data
Brooks, Bruce.
    Dolores : Seven stories about her / Bruce Brooks.
    Summary: A series of events captures the life of a
free-spirited girl as she grows from a savvy seven-year-
old to a self-assured sixteen-year-old.
    ISBN 0-06-027818-8
    ISBN 0-06-029473-6 (lib. bdg.)
    [1. Identity—Fiction. 2. Brothers and sisters—Fiction.]
I. Title.
PZ7.B7913 Dn   2002   2001039435
[Fic]—dc21   CIP
                                              AC

Typography by Amy Ryan
1   2   3   4   5   6   7   8   9   10
❖
First Edition

For Gail Hochman

half good
in black

THE THING IS, OF COURSE, NO ONE WOULD EVER have hung out someplace as tacky as the Wal-Mart if it hadn't been for Jimmy getting the job of ordering CDs for the music department and stocking the coolest music in town. Everyone knew Wal-Mart was for trailer-park lowlifes. You didn't even want your car to be seen driving in the parking lot of the Wal-Mart.

But Jimmy had thought ahead. As soon as he saw the backhoes digging and the little board sign saying WAL-MART IS COMING! he decided to try it. Three weeks before the store opened, he put on a tie and went in to see the manager and just blew

the guy away with all he knew about music—
all kinds of music—especially what kids would
buy. Jimmy even had these graphs he'd cut out of
magazines showing how much money kids spent
on CDs, talking "market share" and all that sort of
thing; the manager not only hired him but pretty
much gave him complete freedom to order anything he thought would interest the coolest kids—
imports, singles, stuff from really small indie
labels, whatever. When he got a look at Jimmy's
ponytail, he did ask that Jimmy check with him
before stocking any CDs with "potentially family-
inappropriate" covers, but otherwise . . .

So everybody started hanging out at (gulp)
Wal-Mart in the evening, especially Fridays, but
only in the music section, and then only in the part
of the music section that Jimmy had created and
entitled NEW MUSIC beneath an officially printed
card just like the other sections—COUNTRY and POP
VOCALS and even ROCK, which was different from
most of the stuff Jimmy's buddies liked. Jimmy
wrote to *AP* and *Magnet* and *Option* and *Wire* and got
them to send him tear sheets of their review sections, so when you read an enticing review in the
copy of *Option* that came in your mail, chances were

good that you would find it waiting for you at Wal-Mart, expensive but immediately available. But of course before you just went and paid for it, you'd want to talk to everybody else about what other reviews you might have missed in zines you didn't see, and it was like some kind of music discussion club, only cool. There were maybe fifteen such musicheads in his crew, and any night, especially Friday, at least nine or ten would be there. Even when Jimmy's shift started late in the evening, the kids were hanging when he arrived.

The manager was pretty mellow about them, considering how strange they looked in the store, scuffing around in baggy skater clothes and crumpled Vans, some with huge jeans, hockey sweaters over hooded sweatshirts, almost all of them carrying a decent crop of zits too, with baseball caps on backward, doo rags, or a lot of hair. To say the least, they didn't fit in among the super-permed peroxide-blond young moms trying not to look like moms, and the poor but proudly spiff minorities. But the kids, raunchy as they may have looked, had jobs after school, and thus money, and music was what they spent it on. An imported Vandals CD live from a concert in Cologne went for twenty-four dollars, a Silvertones collection from a tiny Chapel Hill label was seventeen dollars—and everybody bought three or four discs a week.

Jimmy hung out with them too, on duty and everything, as if he were being a salesman, which in fact he was. Despite being "dressed up" the way all Wal-Mart employees had to be, he looked pretty decent, in his baggy Girbaud khakis and a way-big denim shirt with one of those Perry Ellis "junk" ties or something. Mostly he always knew, way ahead of time, what music to turn them on to, with a specificity that was secretly touching to each of them. He'd hold out a disc and say, "I ordered this for you because I think you'll get into the way the guy stays at home on the low end of the bass," or "Try this out and see if you don't think these two German dudes have outrun techno and are making real music out of found noise the way you've been trying to do with your mobile recordings of machinery and street crowds." Jimmy knew his tunes, but more importantly, he knew his people.

For Jimmy, the only problem was that every Friday night he had to take Dolores with him. His parents had always insisted on "dating" each other regularly, as if this would make them like each other better, and Friday was their favorite night to get a sitter and go out. But since he had turned fifteen, *he* had become the automatic sitter for his seven-year-old sister. He had his own car, an old VW Beetle he had modestly reconditioned himself, and his parents allowed him to take Dolores out instead of keeping her home, as long as everything was safe. And his boss said he could keep his sister with him as long as the CDs kept moving. Dolores, he thought, really was pretty great for a little kid—growing up around him and his friends had made her hip beyond her years, and his friends had come to treat her more or less as an expected part of the whole crowd, half in a mascot sort of way, half as a real participant in whatever was happening. But after all, she *was* only seven, she still needed supervision, so he could never really relax when she was along.

As he drove to the Wal-Mart tonight, Dolores heard "Lithium" come on the radio and asked him to turn it up, and then turn it up *again* until it was really blasting, and she even sang along with the chorus, *"I love you, I'm not gonna crack,"* at the top of her little voice, which he bet no *other* seven-year-old could come close to doing. The next song was an old one by Helmet, and she sang along with that one, too.

There was more to Do than music, of course. Jimmy loved her and wasn't the least bit ashamed of it. He had been there when she was born, he had given her her first bath (it wasn't gross at all), he had coaxed her to take her first steps, he admired to the point of benign envy her confidence and general air of happy kindness. She was a good human. He felt lucky to be so close to her. She even played ice hockey, Jimmy's best sport, as a Mite A on a travel team, not only the only girl on the squad but its best player. Jimmy was an assistant coach on her team, on the ice with the kids for every practice unless *he* had one for his own travel Midget B team at a conflicting time.

At the Wal-Mart they parked and got out and started walking toward the store. Dolores didn't need her hand held in the parking lot or anything like that; she had her hands shoved in the pockets of her little North Face jacket, and she knew perfectly well to watch for cars herself. On the way toward the store she suddenly shouted,

"Hey, Penwick!" to a kid with long blond hair who had been slinking toward the doors. He turned and saw them, and gave them a smile and a wave. It was Ory Penwick, the rhythm guitarist from Jimmy's band, who was also in five of Jimmy's classes at school. Penwick was perhaps Jimmy's best friend; he said, "Yo, Do," to her with a big smile, before they caught up and he lightly tapped knuckles with her brother.

Jimmy was especially glad to see Penwick here. Penwick—a universally liked "nice kid"—was his ally in the band, composing most of the songs with him and helping to keep the lead guitarist/singer and the drummer concentrated on the music at hand; he would be good to have along if either of the other two players were here, which was likely. Carson, the guitarist, and Chance, the drummer, simply didn't seem to be very good-hearted kids, and if they took it into their heads, they could waste an entire practice putting down players in other bands and mocking Jimmy and Penwick for being such goody-goodies about practicing and writing.

Glancing up the music aisle, past the women scrounging for acrylic blouses with spangles and makeup on sale because it had passed its expiration date, Jimmy saw it was a big night for what his crew called "Jimmy's Tune Boutique." Ten kids were already there, including some girls, which always made things interesting. One of them, Jimmy couldn't help noticing, was his former girlfriend Luisa from two years ago, who—he had been informed by a mutual girl friend on the phone—liked him again and wanted to start going out once more. He wasn't sure about it; maybe tonight he'd check it out.

Dolores ran ahead but veered off into a side aisle full of toys. When Jimmy pulled even, she was flipping rapidly through what he thought was a new line of Silver Surfer figures she probably hadn't seen before.

"Come on, Do," he said from the end of the aisle.

Dolores was jostling through the awkwardly racked bubble packs as fast as she expertly could. "Just a sec," she said. "Let me just see if they've got any of the Green—"

"You're making a mess," he said, as four or five bubble packs popped off the rack onto the floor. "Pick those up and come on. We'll stop by on the way out, I promise. Okay?"

Dolores pouted slightly and put the fallen figures back, sneaking as many looks as she could at the figures behind them. She said, "All right, if you promise. But the one I'm looking for is hard to find, and if they have any, they'll probably sell them by then."

"We'll find it for you, don't worry. We always do, don't we, somewhere or other?" Jimmy moved up the main aisle again. Carson greeted him with unusual good cheer and even showed him a disc Jimmy had suggested to Carson two weeks ago, because the bass and lead guitar worked together in octaves and split-time syncopation, which he thought might be something he and Carson could try. Secretly Jimmy was ecstatic. This was the kind of focus his band needed: *musical* ideas, *musical* cooperation, not putdowns about owning the wrong kind of skateboard trucks or having a stupid logo on your cap.

Dolores, as she always did, just plowed into the middle of everything and greeted everyone, and talked music or action figures or whatever the heck she wanted. Jimmy knew his friends looked out for her as much as he did, because they liked her nearly as much and were willing to listen in amusement to her excited, jabbery explanations of meteors or volcanoes, as learned that week in second grade, or to her impassioned claim that the Meat Puppets were better than Nirvana. The kids *respected* her too—that was it. Jimmy heard a general outburst of laughter and was not surprised to see Do gesturing madly at the center of it.

"Hello, James," said a girl's voice behind him. He turned. There, looking him right in the eyes with an expectant, slightly mischievous smile, was Luisa. The *James* was a giveaway—she was the only person who called him that, even including his parents. She had always done so, after he confessed one intimate evening that he secretly preferred it to the inevitable *Jimmy*.

He was a little taken aback by Luisa's boldness. He had imagined that the whole *maybe-back-together-maybe-not* business would be handled by the intermediary who had telephoned him to bring the matter up for thought.

As if she'd read his mind, before he could think of what to say, Luisa spoke again.

"I thought we knew each other well enough to do without the usual game playing. I thought I could just tell you face to face: I haven't found any-body close to being as nice as you were, and I was a dope to let you go. I want to try again." She looked so fiercely earnest, it must have struck her as comic; she suddenly laughed. Her teeth were so white against her roasted-nut-colored skin and black wavy hair that Jimmy's breath caught in his throat. Luisa was half Latina, half Pakistani; her parents, both doctors, had met in a volunteer field hospital after a terrible earthquake in Mexico. For a second Jimmy flashed on having kissed her, and his knees almost gave out.

But he rallied. "You told me 'Nice isn't enough,'" he said, with what he hoped was an arch smile. "You said, 'I want excitement, and I think excite-ment comes from being a little *bad*.'"

Luisa winced. When her eyes closed, Jimmy noticed her incredibly long eyelashes and felt them fluttering against his cheek as she blinked while he held her during some of their long talks; his knees nearly buckled again. She blushed too, checkbones turning dark pink beneath her match-less color.

"Maybe I learned my lesson," she said, but with a little pain cutting her confidence of a moment ago. "Maybe I learned *bad* is nothing but bad." She fixed him with a soulful two-eyed stare that contained pain he did not understand or really want to know about. "And *nice*," she went on, "is nothing but nice."

"Hey, Bassman, you still interested in music or what?" said a male voice behind him, accompanied by a tug on his sleeve that was just a little more forceful than it needed to be.

He turned reluctantly, to find his drummer, Chance. Chance was holding about ten CDs awkwardly splayed in his arms. "I need you to buy a few of these for the band," he told Jimmy. "I'm short the coin."

"For the band," Jimmy repeated, removing the top two and glancing at them. One of them he already owned—an older Replacements CD he had already played so much at band practices that Dolores, who sat through many on a perch behind the drums, had memorized the lyrics to every song.

"Finally ready to *listen* to this?" Jimmy said, immediately regretting that it sounded reproachful. Chance shrugged, but the record then reminded Jimmy of Do. He looked past Chance's

14

shoulder. "Hey—where's Dolores?" he asked out loud of the general group. He scanned his dozen friends; his sister was no longer among them. He was surprised to feel his chest clench in a sudden panic. He didn't stop to think of what he might be afraid of; on some level he had the feeling he might not even know.

"James—" said Luisa.

He turned back to her, looking past *her* shoulder down the main aisle, and held up his hand. "Look, let's talk, really, okay? I mean, I want to, word up. But right now I have to find my sister."

His panic had grown and was something he now had to fight back in order to make the most elementary of moves. Stupidly, for just a second, he found himself *wishing* that Dolores was still visibly with him, as if he were a three-year-old and wishing had any value. He forced himself to trot down the main aisle and swung to face down the side aisle she had scooted into earlier. He fully expected to find her zipping quickly through the action figures, looking for her rare Green Goblin, and he spoke as he turned in, letting his panic waver into anger in his voice.

"Hey, listen, you know better—"

But Dolores wasn't there. The side aisle was occupied solely by a dyed-blond youngish woman, kneeling before the array of figures in a helplessly befuddled manner. She looked up, almost beseechingly, at the sound of his voice.

Trying to seem calm, trying to remember exactly what he should ask about, he said to the woman, "Have you seen a seven-year-old in a black jacket?"

"She left five minutes ago with her aunt," the blonde said matter-of-factly. Then, in a more whiny voice, "But have *you* seen a Green Goblin with a Pumpkin-Bomb Wing-Slinger?"

"What do you mean, 'her aunt'?" Jimmy snapped, his voice breaking on the final, unnatural word. They had no aunts.

"I mean a big lady told me she was her *aunt*," the blonde snapped back. "Two ladies, actually, but only one said—"

"What did they look like?"

"Plain and ugly," said the woman, now angry. "Like Green Goblin, for all I know. He *sounds* ugly as a graveyard dog. Now, will you help me—"

"Sorry," Jimmy managed to say as he turned to start running back up the main aisle. Instead, he ran smack into Luisa, who had followed him, apparently overheard the talk, and was looking at him imploringly.

"Luisa, I can't right now—"

"The doors," she said. "We have to get them to seal the doors."

"What?" Jimmy said, honestly perplexed for a moment.

Luisa looked at him for a half second, then both of them raced back up the aisle. Luisa was the first to push through the door to the store office. By the time Jimmy arrived, she was saying, "—all the exits, emergency ones too. You just have to tell them a child has possibly been snatched."

"Snatched?" said Jimmy, his voice cracking again. Where had she thought *that* up? he thought vaguely, wondering what exactly she had been exposed to during the past two years. Meanwhile, the manager had caught her urgency and run off through another door into the back of the store. Moments later a smooth voice came over the public address system usually used to announce a fifteen-minute special on pantyhose, and said, "Ladies and gentlemen, Wal-Mart shoppers, we regret any inconvenience, but at this time we must seal off the exits from the store and request that no one attempt to leave the premises. Our telephones will be placed at your disposal if you need to make any calls to say you may be a few minutes late for your next appointment, but we hope the matter will not take more than a minute or two to resolve." Voices all over the store were raised in anger, and as if to assuage them, the announcer continued, "The matter, ladies and gentlemen, concerns the safety of a *child*."

Jimmy took Luisa's arm and turned her to face him. For some reason—maybe, he realized, because he didn't want to face what she thought might be happening—he tried to pull off a big calm-guy act. "Hey," he said with a smile, "this is too much—she's probably just over in the stuffed animals—Do is too smart to go off with a stranger—"

Luisa said, "She's *seven*, James. She could be halfway to the airport by now, then on a plane to Seattle or Hong Kong or Miami, okay? Okay?"

"Okay," he heard himself gulp.

"Come on," Luisa said. They ran though some double doors that led to the true rear of the store—boxes of merchandise stacked to the ceiling, loading dock visible through huge doors, staff locker rooms and bathrooms.

Luisa and Jimmy arrived at the door of a staff ladies' room. "In here," Luisa said, and pushed through the door, yanking him with her.

"Wait—" he said. But he was inside before he knew it.

A tall woman teetered on one foot before the mirror, putting on perhaps her twelfth pair of tights. She screamed. "Thief," snarled Luisa, then bent and looked under the stall doors.

"Nothing," she said. Then Luisa found another staff bathroom way in the rear of the stock delivery area. As soon as they walked in, Jimmy saw it was dirtier than the others, but more than that, he felt something dreadful in the air. So, evidently, did Luisa.

"Ah," she said. Then she bent, stood, and ran over to the third stall, the largest, marked with a wheelchair sign. She pointed at the door. "Kick that in," she said.

When Jimmy, somewhat confused, hesitated, she clicked her tongue, reared back on one leg, and kicked hard at the door herself. Her second kick blasted it open. They both stood for an instant and looked inside.

There were three people in the stall, all looking at them in surprise at being interrupted. Sitting on the closed toilet, wearing a pink dress that was not her own and a pink parka from which the tags still dangled, was Dolores. Around her shoulders was a flowered towel spotted with black stains; half of her sandy hair was dyed an artificially deep black.

Standing beside and a little behind her was a plain-looking woman of about thirty-five, holding a rag to a bottle of black hair dye. On the other side stood another plain woman, slightly younger. She held Dolores's shoulders tightly.

"I'm getting what you call a *makeover*," Dolores said, trying to sound chipper. But Jimmy could hear the fear in her voice, as if things had gone way beyond what she might have expected.

They were all frozen for a second, but then as if on some signal the woman with the dye threw the bottle's contents into Luisa's eyes while the other woman pushed Do to the floor behind the toilet. Jimmy's eyes followed his sister, which allowed both women to dash by Luisa, who was cursing and slinging liquid from her face, and run into him squarely in the solar plexus with their elbows and shoulders. In a second they were past him and headed for the door.

"Get them!" screamed Luisa.

Jimmy, his horror forgotten, took two low steps and launched himself into a horizontal leap that let him snag the hindmost woman's ankles in his arms. She went down with a surprised yelp, like a punt returner who thought he'd seen daylight ahead, and struck her head hard against a sink. She crumpled to the floor without another sound and lay still. Her partner paused a half second to look back, then lit out on her own.

Letting go of the unconscious woman, Jimmy jumped to his feet. He looked back. Luisa cradled Do's mottled head; Dolores was starting to let herself go, beginning to sob.

"Do—" Jimmy took a step toward them.

"I've got her okay," said Luisa quickly. She pointed at the door. "Get that bitch." He stood uncertainly for another second. "*Get* her!" Luisa snarled.

Jimmy ran. After making two quick lefts, he saw the second woman ahead; she snapped her head over her shoulder and saw him, too. She dodged around a forklift loaded with a huge stack of boxes marked FISHER-PRICE. As she passed, she swatted them down behind her so they tumbled into his path. He jumped to the side of the cascade and looked ahead. She was making for a fire door thirty feet away.

The forklift was still idling, but the driver had braked it and vaulted clear once he saw the trouble.

Now, it just so happened that when he had been Dolores's age, Jimmy had been fascinated by the forklifts that openly worked the aisles at Home Depot; in fact, more than once he had been momentarily "lost" to his mother as he followed them around, absorbing every detail of their operation at the hands of their drivers.

He sprang into the seat of this one now, jammed it into forward gear, turned its steering wheel in an arc gentle enough to avoid tipping it, and ran it straight through the pile of boxes, pushing them before it like snow before a snowplow, to intercept the fleeing woman. A box caught at her heels and she fell, but on her knees she still tried to crawl to the door, now less than ten feet away. Without a moment's hesitation, Jimmy, who had slowed at her fall, speeded up again. Another couple of boxes laid her flat, and Jimmy drove the heavy forklift on its small wheels to within a foot of her knees and upper legs. He pulled the gear lever back into neutral.

"Move and you lose your legs," he shouted, in a high voice he thought sounded anything but mean. So he revved the engine for menace. The woman, wailing something, did not move.

Three security guards popped through the door from the store and ran toward them. Not really sure what he was doing, Jimmy jumped down from the forklift and bent close to the woman's ear. She was just gasping wildly now. She smelled like a sour towel.

Now that he was so close, Jimmy could think of nothing sharp to say. He looked up and saw Luisa and Dolores standing beyond a jumble of boxes, neither of them crying anymore, both watching. He bent back to the woman's ear. "She's my *sister*," he said. "My *sister*."

The police showed up then. One of them found Dolores's clothes stuffed in a trash can inside the bathroom. A man in a brown suit photographed Do, Luisa, Jimmy, the bad women, and everything in the area a thousand times. A young woman in uniform took the two kidnappers away in an ambulance followed by a patrol car. Eventually, a large man in a tweedy sports coat and rumpled corduroys told Luisa, Dolores, and Jimmy—in a kind voice that nevertheless held some iron authority—that they could go back to their friends.

Before the three of them got to the doors, Jimmy stopped Luisa and Dolores and took his sister into a shaking hug.

"God, Do," he said, beginning to cry, "God, I'm sorry, I'm so sorry—"

Dolores was crying too. "No, Jimmy, I was stupid, the tall one said she was a distant aunt, I *know* we don't have any, but she said she could make me so pretty—"

"No, *I'm* the idiot—"

"No, Jimmy, it was *me*—"

"You're *both* fools," said Luisa harshly. *"Fools!* And I hope you were both scared half to death."

Jimmy and Dolores let go of each other just enough to turn and stare at Luisa. Then Do, still sobbing, began to laugh. Jimmy found himself unable to resist joining her. Soon Luisa, trying to frown ferociously, started as well.

Once the bizarre laughter ended, the three of them pushed through the doors and saw their friends. Only Chance had left; the rest were waiting nervously, and burst into applause as Dolores reappeared. She skipped over, starting to chatter, and they closed into a circle around her. On the way to join them, Jimmy asked Luisa to marry him. She declined, but indicated that she was free for a movie tomorrow night.

"I'd think it over, if I were you, this marriage offer," said Jimmy. "I mean, you're not going to hook too many nice guys when you look like a carny's bad toy raccoon."

"The dye will come off," she said.

"You hope."

"It will come off, I *hope*, at about the same time you learn what it means to be responsible for your sister."

Jimmy slowed, said nothing for a moment, then took a deep breath. "All right," he said, "I certainly deserve that, one time, from you. I will hear it for the rest of my life from my parents and everyone else in my family. But listen: nobody— *nobody*—is going to have the dreams I will have for the rest of my life. And if *you* ever make that comment again to me, now that you've used your single opportunity, then I will leave you wherever we are, and never see you again, which may not seem like much of a threat but is the best I can do."

She thought for a second. "Fair enough," she said. "And are you finished with your self-pity now?" Jimmy nodded. Luisa took his hand.

Dolores was being assured that her half-black hair job was cutting-edge alterna-rock low fashion, and before Jimmy left with her, she was allowed to browse through the action figures for as long as she liked. When she found the one she wanted, a crewcut man wearing a white, short-sleeved shirt, a thin black tie, and a badge that said MANAGER refused to let Jimmy pay for it. "I'm the one made the call to secure the area," he said. Jimmy thanked him, and was a bit ashamed of noting that the man's tie was a clip-on.

However, as they made their way out the front door, the manager followed them all the way to the car. Jimmy let Dolores in, buckled her seat belt as she ripped her figure from the bubble-packed card, then crossed behind the car toward the driver's side. The crewcut man, standing with his feet apart, smelling of Old Spice, blocked Jimmy's path.

"Excuse me," said Jimmy, making as if to step around the man.

But the man stepped with him, remaining in his way, then poked him in the chest with a forefinger. "If that was *my* little girl and you let her get kidnapped—"

Jimmy backhanded the man's finger away and said, "—then you'd shoot me with your bird gun and go to jail and have *no* kids anymore. Wonderful. Love, love, love, everywhere. Look," he said, poking the plainly surprised man with his own forefinger, "if that *were* your little girl, maybe she'd be back in your stuffy apartment eating Doritos in place of dinner and watching reruns of *Ren and Stimpy*, instead of meeting interesting people with her older brother and making friends. And, yes, putting herself in the path of danger because her stupid brother let himself get distracted for a few minutes." He breathed into the man's face. "I learned what I needed to learn tonight, and so did she. Having you come on all heavy and try to teach it to us again like some moral bully is *totally* redundant, okay? Now— thank you for sealing the doors, I mean it, and thanks for the action figure, and *excuse me.*"

He walked around the man, got into his car, and drove off.

"If I'd had Green Goblin's Pumpkin-Bomb Wing-Slinger, those bad ladies would have been total *toast*," said Dolores, fooling with her brightly colored plastic things as they drove. *"Bavoooom!"* she said, presumably imitating a pumpkin bomb. Jimmy saw that her hands were still shaking.

"You had Luisa," said Jimmy. "She's better than Green Goblin. And those ladies *are* toast now, anyway. And you know what? You don't need to let anyone try to make you pretty. You're pretty all by yourself."

At the next stoplight, Dolores reached up and wrenched the rearview mirror so she could study her appearance. After turning her face this way and that, she said, "You're right. I look *good* in black."

"You look *half* good in black," Jimmy tried to correct her, twisting the mirror back as the light changed.

"No," she said. "To be absolutely correct, I look good in *half* black. *Very* good."

He laughed. "Have it your way."

"I will," she said.

dad, missing,
not missing

FROM THE BEDROOM IN THE REAR OF THE APARTMENT, Jimmy heard the snap of the alarm mechanism popping up on his father's plastic clock in the living room down the hall. As usual, no alarm followed; his father had woken up and disarmed the buzz or bell or whatever signal it was before it could chirp. Jimmy realized something weird: I've spent four nights a week here for nine months and I still don't know what kind of noise that alarm is supposed to make.

"Jimmy?" came the sleepy voice of Dolores from across the dark room.

"What is it?" whispered Jimmy. "You're supposed to be asleep."

"So are you," she said. "Jimmy, why does he do that?"

"Do what?"

She sighed. "You know what I mean. Stop the alarm."

"Whatever his reason is," said Jimmy, "he's pretty quick with the hand."

"That, or he ain't been asleep."

"Don't say *ain't*."

"Don't change the subject."

They were quiet for a moment as the sounds of pans carefully handled came from the kitchen.

"Bet it's eggs," said Dolores, "with cheese. I hope he uses American."

"That's not even really cheese," said Jimmy. He wasn't whispering anymore.

"Whatever. So—why does he stop the alarm? If it was me, I'd have to let it buzz away until I couldn't stand not to wake up."

"'If it *were* me,'" Jimmy said.

A controlled sizzle came from the kitchen. Then, very faintly, strains of instrumental music.

"Man's got to have his tunes," said Dolores.

"Man runs on music," Jimmy said.

"So," said Do, "why does Man snip off alarm?"

Jimmy sighed. "Obviously because he doesn't want to wake us."

"So we can get, what, fifteen more minutes' sleep?"

They heard a fork whipping something in a bowl.

"Right," said Jimmy. "I guess to him the extra fifteen minutes is worth the effort."

"Fifteen minutes for *us*," Dolores said.

"Right," Jimmy said. "For us. *Always* for us."

"Don't get all mushy. We're his kids. He's *supposed* to take care of us."

Jimmy looked over at her side of the room. The world was growing slightly, slowly less opaque in its shadows. She had her hands behind her head as she lay on her back. Jimmy thought she looked a lot older than eight.

He said, "Pierce could do a lot less and still 'take care of us' just fine."

"Why do you call him 'Pierce'?"

"It's his name."

"I call him 'Daddy.'"

"You're a suck-up."

A pillow flew through the air like a raven's ghost and landed smack on Jimmy's head. Jimmy could just make out the large figure of Spider-Man. "Why?" Dolores said.

Jimmy put the pillow behind his head. "I don't know. I guess he always had this identity as, you know, himself, as a guy. And I guess that *then*, when he went on from there and was completely no one but my father—you know, helping me like collect Hot Wheels and knowing all the car names, or hockey cards and knowing all the tough ones to find, and playing all kinds of stuff, making sure I learned to kick as well with my left foot in soccer as with my right—I felt even more how far he had to come from just being a selfish Pierce dude."

Dolores said nothing for a moment. Then, out of the shadow, "Pure mush."

Something popped loudly in the kitchen.

"Oh boy," Dolores said, *"bacon!"*

"No doubt the nitrite-free kind."

"Yeah, but at least he doesn't tell us we're going to die of cancer if we eat nitrites, *any* nitrites, the way Mom does."

Jimmy laughed. "Hey, we'd be dead by *now*."

Dolores was quiet. Then she said, "Think she'd really care?"

"Dolores!"

"Come on, *you* know, there's always a kind of gleam in her eye. 'You'll *die* if you eat bacon!' 'You'll *die* if you drink diet sodas!' 'You'll *die* if you eat fast-food french fries!' I mean, all this dying. It *would* make it pretty easy for them to just, like, break up, if we disappeared. I mean, *we* are what's making it complicated and all."

Jimmy thought. "But no matter what there is between them, Do, they both still *love* us," he said. As he spoke, they heard the sound of a quiet blender from the kitchen.

"Smoothies," Dolores said. "I hope they're not too thick. Low on the bananas, if we're lucky."

Jimmy said, "He bought that blender because it had the quietest motor."

"Quiet, quiet. Sleep, sleep," she said. "All this time we're supposed to be sacking it out."

"Well," said Jimmy, sounding surprised, "yes. What's wrong with that?"

"I don't know. Nothing, I guess. Except we're *not* asleep."

"That ain't his fault." He laughed. "He kept *me*

35

up late, made me write my whole French essay over."

"Oh, *please* say *ain't*," she said. Then: "How come? The French?"

"Oh," he said with a yawn, "I was lazy the first time, and he knew when he read it."

"You're pretty lazy now," said Dolores.

In the kitchen, the toaster made its springy sound.

"Pop-Tarts," said Dolores, "or English muffins?"

"Pop-Tarts. Definitely. I can hear the *weight*."

"We got about four more minutes before he wakes us and takes us out to the complete breakfast set on the table all nice and ready," Dolores said. "What I want to know is, is there anything else he does? I mean, he'll take us to drop you off, that's almost an hour, then he'll take me to the Bagelrama to get me a cinnamon-raisin and let me use the bathroom, then drop *me* at school, pick me up later, play with me until you have to go to hockey practice, and back, while I freeze my butt off at the rink, then cook dinner, play more with me until *The Simpsons*, then, like, homework with you or something, for sure *I* don't know, then you go to bed late. And, what? He lies down on his lumpy futon and listens to Duke Ellington on his earphones?"

"I guess," said Jimmy, suddenly feeling uneasy.

"You *guess*," said Dolores. "Well, I *guess* too. But I don't feel bad about it."

"You don't?" said Jimmy.

They heard the sound of things being scraped onto plates. Twice.

"Now the music will go up," said Dolores.

The music went up. It was jazz piano.

Footsteps came down the hall.

"You think he *likes* all this?" Jimmy asked, in spite of himself.

Jimmy heard a rustling in Dolores's bed as the footsteps drew near the door. "I think he likes *us*," whispered Dolores. "Now, pretend you're *asleep*! It's the least we can do."

Jimmy closed his eyes and lay still. The room was quiet as the door opened.

do they
        mean it?

THE FOUR GIRLS STOOD TOGETHER IN A ROUGH circle, their frosty breaths colliding in the circle's center, as if their intention was to create a small, complex cloud.

"I mean, like, check her *out*," said one, a large girl in an oversized Philadelphia Eagles Starter coat. She was looking over the shoulder of the girl across from her, and the girls on either side of her followed her eyes. The girl across did not turn around. Eagle Coat snorted, as if to retrieve her last contribution to the cloud. "I mean, a *yo-yo*! Get real!"

"She's real," said the girl who hadn't turned,

"and so's the yo-yo. I bet she's even very *good*."

"Whatever *that* means," said another girl, this one wearing a short jacket with a torso of black plastic that looked like patent leather, with blue denim sleeves.

"It means she can probably do all kinds of tricks with her yo-yo, and there *are* tricks, believe me. You *can* be 'good' at yo-yo," said the girl who wouldn't turn.

"Who does it get you?" said the last girl, much more quietly than the first two. She watched too, but where the others fidgeted with their eyes as if searching for something to feel, she watched calmly. She wore a burgundy parka without any logos on it.

"Anybody weird," snorted Eagle Coat.

"Anybody who *likes* weirdos," said Two-tone.

"That's what I just *said*."

"No," said the girl who wouldn't turn. She wore a plain, traditional jean jacket, one sleeve covered with iron-on patches saying PRONG and TOOL and PANTERA and SLAYER. "You both said different things. There are weirdos, and there are people who aren't weird but who *like* weirdos. You can be both at once, but you don't have to be."

"Which kind is Dolores?" asked the quiet girl.

At last the girl in the patched jacket pivoted at the waist—she couldn't go so far as to move her feet—and took a look across the playground. It was a pretty long look. When she turned back, she resumed her study of the frosty-breath cloud. Not once had she looked at any of the other girls, but now she flicked her eyes around the circle and made quick contact with each.

"Maybe we should find out," she said.

Eagle Coat snorted. "Who needs to? She's a weirdo for sure."

"How do we find out?" asked the quiet girl.

"Easy. Real easy. We just torture her for a while," said Patch Jacket.

Nobody had anything to add.

Meanwhile, across the cold playground, by herself in a spot that fell in the tattersall shadow of the ancient lead-pipe jungle gym, Dolores concentrated on keeping her clear red Duncan Imperial spinning on its axis long enough for her to rock the cradle. She tried again and again, with the yo-yo slowing and stopping just as she got the string cradle set up. She never kept it going quite long enough this morning, and when the bell rang, she sighed, gave the yo-yo a couple of quick, hard down-and-ups, then, timing it just right, slipped the string off her finger as the yo-yo was coming up, let it climb past her face into the air until the string had been completely wound up, held open a side pocket of her wool Navy-surplus peacoat, and let the spinning yo-yo fall neatly into it.

"At least I can do *that*," she muttered. Then she picked up her book sack and headed for the school building.

Across the playground, Eagle Coat snorted. "Show-off," she said.

"Of course, dummy," snapped Patch Jacket. "What else do you stand around doing yo-yo in public *for*? The whole *idea* is to show off."

Nobody said anything. Slowly, regretfully, the girls straggled in toward the building. They did not carry book sacks or, indeed, books. They were the last ones in.

But it was proving more difficult than the four girls anticipated to find a way to torture the girl they had dubbed "Her Weirdness." Their first attempt was to spread a rumor that Dolores's considerable breasts were in fact surgically implanted, displayed in their full deceitfulness purely to draw the lust of the seventh grade's boys. This rumor incited some satisfactory resentment among other girls, but it never seemed either to reach Dolores's attention or to affect her mildly distracted air of barely acknowledging that she had a human body at all. The rumor finally broke down after repeated showers following gym class—showers in which Dolores lingered longer than anyone, singing old Beatles songs to herself, seemingly lost to the world—gave every other girl the chance to see that the breasts consisted unmistakably of flesh moving naturally. Besides, Dolores showed no special sexual interest in boys; mostly, she seemed to seek them out only to have them show her the arcane yo-yo tricks of which they were masters, or to swap with her the graphic novels they too collected.

Next, a rumor made the rounds that Dolores was a lesbian "in love" with Ms. Dukakis, the gorgeous algebra teacher who, despite being watched ardently by almost everyone for two years, had never been seen in the company of a man. However, once more the rumor seemed not to get through to its victim; in fact, in the middle of its run, Dolores actually *encouraged* the whole idea by seeking private after-school help with Ms. Dukakis herself for three weeks. It was not the sort of distancing I'll-show-you-it's-not-true nervousness that the architects of the torture expected. They were perplexed. This Dolores girl was either crazy or fearless, both of which would make further attempts to injure her through rumor very difficult. Shelly, the patch-jacket leader of the foursome, interpreted Dolores's blithe extra-help sessions as a devil-may-care back slap, straight from Dolores to her and her pitiful slander.

Which, in fact, it was. One day before phys. ed. Shelly was surprised to find herself suddenly alone with Dolores in an aisle of the locker room, and even more surprised when Dolores said, "Well, Shelleroo, what'll it be next?"

"Excuse me?" Shelly managed to stammer as she watched Dolores tighten the shoestrings of a sneaker.

Without looking up, Dolores said, "Fake titties first, then the supposedly repugnant, dark mysteries of dykedom—I'm curious about what's coming next. Are you going to try suggesting I'm a vampire? I'd probably have heck of a time with that. How about maybe I was born a boy but had that surgery in Sweden when I was three or four? No, no—on second thought, maybe it's best if you surprise me."

"I don't know what you're talking about." Shelly was proud of herself for being able to huff convincingly.

Dolores knotted her second sneaker and stood up. "No," she said cheerfully, "you just don't know what *you* are talking about. But keep it up."

Shelly tried. She masterminded two more campaigns—one vaguely sexual, involving the male science teacher and the collection of lab rats he kept in his room, the other purely academic (a daring, desperate departure into strange territory for Shelly and her pals), involving constant plagiarism from a genius wild girl supposedly held captive in a distant shed. But the menace was obliquely deflected by Dolores (for example, she snuck her cat, Buzz, into science class for a week; three rats disappeared; the teacher banished the girl from the room for two weeks). Shelly, in her turn, sought out Dolores, again in an aisle of the locker room.

"Dolores," Shelly said sternly, "we need to talk."

"Hey, Shelfonzo. Loved the rats bit—oooooh." Dolores gave a shiver.

"Damn it, what *are* you afraid of?" Shelly asked—not defeated, maybe, but certainly dry of formulaic malice. "Don't you care what people say about you?"

"Not in the least," said Dolores. "That should have been obvious from the start, Shelly. I *do* care what people *feel* about me, a very *few* people, and certainly not ones who are likely to feel different because they think I might be wearing silicone in my tits. As for what I'm afraid of . . . " She seemed to think about it seriously for almost a minute, time enough for Shelly to try to revive her enmity by noticing that Dolores was, apparently without effort, both strange looking and astonishingly beautiful.

"Termites," Dolores finally said.

"Termites?"

"Yeah. The bugs that eat wood. I saw this special on TV when I was about six, and ever since, I've been afraid that while we are all going around my mother's house acting jolly and ignorant, these secret little jaws are gnawing away behind the walls, until one day—*phwoom!*—the house just collapses around us. *That's* what I fear. So now you know."

Shelly shook her head. "You *are* weird."

Dolores sighed. "Oh, come *on*, Shelster! You can do better than that. I mean, this is the *seventh grade!* I've been hearing 'weird' and 'weirdo' since *kindergarten*. That's eight years, Shel. After eight years, a word can kind of lose its punch, you know?"

"How about if I tell you you're messed up?"

"Better." Dolores nodded. "Kind of broad, but certainly less common. First heard it in second grade. It stuck around for a few years, then just seemed to fall out of fashion. I don't believe anyone has called me 'messed up,' nice and simple like that, without profanity, for—jeez—" She wrinkled her forehead and looked at the ceiling. "It must be three years now."

"You think you're so cool."

"As a matter of fact, you have absolutely no idea what I think," Dolores said. "But if you'll allow me to rephrase that comment in the form of a question, the answer is that in fact I do *not* think I am 'so cool' in the least. For all I know, I *may* be cool, or perhaps I may be irretrievably nerdy. But that's for other, wiser, trendier minds to decide."

Shelly pressed on. "Why are you always doing stuff other people don't do? Why are you alone so much?"

Dolores winced, and looked genuinely wounded for an instant. "Well," she said, with a half smile and the obvious flaring of something that Shelly didn't think was quite anger, but certainly wasn't indifference, either, "Shelly, old buddy, why don't you just tell *me*?"

"What's that supposed to mean? How am I supposed to—"

"Because, see, *you* are the expert on why I'm alone so much. That's right. Because you—or people you represent—are the very ones who *leave* me alone. Check it out for yourself. There you are, on the playground before school. And there, twenty feet away, am I. Do you ever walk over and start a conversation with weird old Dolores, even an inane one, when she's standing over there by herself doing something harmless or even harmlessly peculiar? No, you do not come over. Instead, with *other* people, you stand nearby and take the trouble to plot my downfall. I'm jigged if

I understand it. Is it my clothes? I have trouble with that—seems too superficial. Is it body odor? Do I fart a lot? Are my teeth mossy without my knowledge? What?"

It was Shelly's turn to ponder. "I think—" she started, then hesitated.

"Yes?" said Dolores encouragingly.

"I think nobody understands you. They think you're—strange, so they're, like, scared."

"Ah." Dolores nodded. Keeping such obvious control of herself that Shelly could detect a tremble in her hand, Dolores said calmly, "So, instead of coming over and asking a direct question, you all hang back and plan campaigns of malicious rumors aimed at hurting me. Have I got it right?"

"Pretty much," said Shelly. "But you forgot to mention—not forgot, really, because you couldn't really know, but anyway—you didn't include in there the fact that, well, personally, I'm just plain mean."

"Gotcha," said Dolores with a nod.

"I don't know why," said Shelly, shifting from one foot to the other. "I've always been mean. It's always made me feel—kind of powerful, like."

"Meanness is *very* powerful," said Dolores. "You

are indeed correct about that. You don't *get* much more powerful than mean."

"Well," said Shelly, "there it is."

"There it is," echoed Dolores, with another small sigh. "I'm weird, and you're mean." She looked up. "But—do we have to, like, point ourselves at each other like missiles? I presume you're not interested in a program of destruction that actually involves *action*—a fistfight, say, or a wrestling match? Even some kind of competition—darts, footrace, skeet shooting?"

Shelly shook her head. "No, I work only by, you know, *talking*." Then, after thinking, she went on. "So you're asking why we— if, like, you could be weird in one direction, and I could be mean in another? To, like, somebody else?"

Dolores nodded. "Somebody who will give you a better value for your efforts. You have to admit, so far, the attempts at 'contact' with me haven't led to much satisfaction, have they?"

Shelly shook her head and considered. "You're saying, like, I've been wasting my time—"

"Your *meanness*, rather."

"Right. That." Shelly thought about it.

"If I may say so, it's not doing much to your

benefit, aimed as it is. Nor is my weirdness attract-
ing you to become a brave, curious friend."

"No," said Shelly with a shiver of her own, "no,
it's not."

"So—"

"Okay," said Shelly, letting out a big breath.
She nodded and looked up and around. "I got to
find somebody I can do some damage to."

"Well, to be honest, I'd rather you didn't try to
damage *anyone*," said Dolores. "But I guess this is
one of those times when I need to look after myself
first." She shrugged.

Shelly felt a weight of futility lift from the back
of her neck. She looked at Dolores dubiously. "Do
we have to, like, shake on it or something?"

"That's not necessary," said Dolores, "though of
course if you like—"

"No, we'll just declare it's all over," Shelly hastened to say. "I won't try to torture you. I won't try
to like you, either, but I won't start any more—
stories."

"Fair enough. And I won't try to intrigue you."

"Never happen," snorted Shelly.

"No," said Dolores, "you're probably right
about that."

Shelly walked away. The next day word got around that Linda Starnes, a plain-looking, straight-A student, was the mother of a child of mixed race whom she kept locked up in a distant shed. At lunchtime Linda was seen to leave the cafeteria weeping. But at recess Dolores finally sustained enough spin on her red Duncan Imperial to rock the cradle for at least three or four seconds, which counted.

ladies
for lunch

It was time for Jenny to set the table, so she finally had to reveal the news to Lorinda.

"We're to be honored today with the presence of my daughter," she said, setting the teal-colored cotton place mats around the circular oak table.

Lorinda, who was sitting in the living room flipping through a catalogue, looked up and raised her eyebrows. "To what do we owe this honor?"

Jenny, placing silverware, laughed. "Maybe she's hungry."

Lorinda laughed as well. "As significant and profound as that?" she said.

Jenny went to the stove to stir the squash soup.

"I have no reason to suppose it's anything *more* significant. From *her* side, at least. From *my* side, of course, I love her. She *is* my daughter." She looked up from the stove, but not at Lorinda. "I *mean* that, you know."

"Of course," Lorinda hastened to agree. "I mean, naturally. It goes without saying."

"I wonder," said her friend, stirring. "Maybe it needs saying."

Lorinda looked down at her hands in silence; obviously *she* wasn't going to say it.

"Well—how about a glass of Piesporter Michelsberg?" said Jenny.

"I thought you'd never ask," said Lorinda, sounding relieved, dropping the catalogue, and rising from the couch.

Jenny poured two glasses of white wine into the only two wineglasses on the table, and the women sat down casually at their places and sipped.

"Wonderful," said Lorinda. Then, "Are you planning on calling Dolores to watch us slurp this fabulous stuff up, to torture her?"

Jenny looked genuinely shocked. "Why should I torture my daughter?"

Lorinda smiled nervously and took another, longer sip. "You tell me?" she said weakly.

They sipped their wine. Then Lorinda said, "Whatever happened to those outbursts of hers, those 'All you do is put on fancy three-hour lunches for your friends instead of working, just so Daddy has to stay up all night writing books to support everybody?' and similar rhetoric we have heard over the years?"

"I'm afraid she got her father's manners," Jenny said. "Now she gets many of his opinions as well."

"I daresay you're right." Lorinda seemed slightly hasty to agree. "But what about your daughter's obvious love of her own originality? Don't you agree Dolores would be too proud just to repeat someone else's opinion?"

Jenny thought as she topped off their glasses. "You may be right," she said. "It's hard to believe a girl of—what must she have been when she said all that? Ten? Nine?—how a girl of that age could come up with such an indictment on her own. But I believe it of Do. She's that sharp." Jenny sighed. "That *smart*."

"You evidently don't suspect her brother of feeding her lines."

Jenny shook her head. "Jimmy keeps his own counsel. Besides, he is probably always at *ice* hockey practice or *lacrosse* practice or at a practice for *some* incredibly important sport."

"Or college."

"Or college, thank you. There is that—he may have been *quite* removed. Anyway, if it wasn't Pierce, it must have been Dolores's own admittedly *somewhat* childish interpretation of events." She smiled wryly. "Wouldn't it be difficult to say whose interpretation would be more childish—that of Pierce at forty-five, or that of Dolores at nine?"

"You could try asking me," said a voice, and Dolores walked into the kitchen, wearing blue jeans and a well-washed scarlet T-shirt that bore the logo of the Detroit Red Wings hockey team, a white wheel with a white wing flowing back from it. She walked straight to the stove and picked up the wooden spoon with which her mother had been stirring the soup.

She stirred it herself, then reached and slightly cut the gas beneath the pot. "It's sticking," she said. "It's a little thick. Hi, Lorinda."

"You can leave the cooking to me, Dolores," said her mother, getting up and moving to the stove. Dolores shrugged, handed her the spoon, and walked over to drop into the place set for her across from Lorinda.

She said, "So. Is your daughter at Stanford yet?"

With some control, Lorinda forced a small laugh and said, "No, actually Jennifer is doing quite well in her—well—"

"Her genius program," Dolores finished the sentence. "Trig in the sixth grade. Whew."

"And I hope *you* are enjoying the ninth grade?" said Lorinda.

"Well, we're still learning our colors," said Dolores. "I'm in eighth. Has ol' Jennifer taken the SATs yet? The chemistry achievement test? Bet she got more than seven hundred."

"Dolores, be civil."

"All right, all right," said Dolores, toying with her forks. After a moment, she held one up and said, "Is this a salad fork or a pie fork? Officially."

Her mother looked over. "That is a pie fork. See the extra protrusion of the outer tine?"

"Goody. What kind of pie are we having?"

"We're not having pie," her mother sighed.

"Then why do we have— Never mind," said Dolores.

Jenny served the soup.

"Which spoon do I use?" asked Dolores.

"Dolores," said Jenny sternly.

"Mom, there are four spoons here! I'm really *asking*! Which one do I use now? God forbid I eat a thick soup with the bouillon spoon or something reserved for thin broths—help me out!"

Lorinda came to the rescue. "The big one," she said, picking up her own.

"Thank you," said Dolores. "And please notice, Mom, how I retain my awareness of propriety by scooping *away* from myself in filling this large implement with this delicious brew."

"Duly noted, Dolores, and *much* appreciated. There's a special place for you in Manners Heaven."

"Indeed there is," said Dolores, and the three of them ate their soup in silence, except for the moment when Dolores whispered, "Isn't it nice how none of us clanks against the bottom of the bowl?"

Once the soup was finished, Dolores asked her mother if she might help by clearing the rim-soup plates as her mom saw to the next course, Cornish game hens stuffed with wild rice, which needed to be removed from the oven. Her mother said she would appreciate the assistance, and Dolores whisked the dishes away, always from the right, without incident or clatter.

However, she declined a game hen when her mother held one above her plate between two large spoons.

"But it's the main course!" Jenny said, with the small nut-brown bird body poised in midair.

"No, *thank* you," Dolores repeated.

"But what on earth is wrong with a game hen? Or are you just being contrary?"

"I am not. And I'd rather not explain the reasons for my perfectly ladylike refusal."

"Well, young lady, you *will* explain," said Jenny.

"Jenny, maybe we ought to—" interjected Lorinda.

"Tell me!" said Jenny.

"All right, then," said Dolores, perfectly composed. "I can't stand the way their tiny little bones shatter when you eat them. Is that sufficient?"

"It is," said Jenny, looking slightly pale. She then served the bird meant for Dolores to Lorinda, who regarded it rather askance in the middle of her huge dinner plate. In the ensuing silence she ate nothing but the small pieces of breast meat, which involved no breaking of bones.

"What's dessert?" Dolores asked with apparently restored relish, as soon as her mother put down her knife and fork, leaving a completely denuded skeleton on her plate.

"Several kinds of delicious cheese," said Jenny.

"What is this, a Dorothy Sayers novel?" said Dolores. "Come on! We live in the United States! We eat *sweets* for dessert."

"Let me recommend just trying the cheese," said Lorinda. "We've rather gotten in the habit of it, and I promise you'll find it a refreshing way to finish."

"Good for you," said Dolores, pushing back her chair and getting up. "But no, thanks. I'll go back to my room and raid my stash of Zero bars. But thanks for the soup, Mom. It was really good."

"You're certainly welcome," said Jenny coolly. "And thank you for joining us."

"You're certainly welcome," said Dolores as she left. "It beats working for a living."

"*Dolores!*"

"Jenny! Please, just let her go," pleaded Lorinda. Dolores clomped up the stairs. Jenny, standing and staring after her, seemed to sag a little. Nodding, she moved to the kitchen counter.

After carefully setting out two antique dessert plates, she brought to the table a small rattan tray covered with broad-leaf lettuces, upon which four kinds of cheeses rested along with a pie slice.

"Oh, God," she said, collapsing into her chair.

"I wish she and Jennifer would be friends," said Lorinda. "Jennifer is so much less—resistant to what one might call enjoying the arts of feminine life."

"You mean she's a normal, smart girl."

"Well—with certain extreme capabilities, yes."

"Whereas Dolores, at thirteen, has the wart-nosed broom-riding thing down pat."

"Well, she certainly knows how to push *your* buttons."

Jenny, forehead in one hand and the pie slice, bearing a slab of Stilton, in the other, dumped the cheese onto her plate and shook her head, "Why does she side with Pierce so relentlessly?"

"Because he's weak," Lorinda said confidently. "And she senses he needs her help. Whereas you are strong even without her, and she doesn't feel she is required to make you whole."

"But I *do* need her. I *love* her!" She shook her head again. "I can't win."

"Honey," said Lorinda, placing her hand on Jenny's forearm, "I'm afraid you already lost, big-time, when you married that feeb, and took his blood into your children's."

Jenny poked at her Stilton. She said, "Dolores would remind me that, technically, Pierce paid for this cheese."

Lorinda made a show of looking around the room. "Funny, I don't see Dolores *or* her father anywhere around, yet you are allowing them to dictate how you regard your dessert."

Jenny laughed and ate a small piece of Stilton. "You're right," she said, chewing. "I have to resist the tendency to internalize their critiques—"

"—in the name of a completely false compassion," Lorinda said. "Of course, I don't mean 'false' in the sense that— God, what was *that*?"

She had been cut off by an elephantine noise coming from upstairs. "Oh, it's just Dolores," Jenny said wearily, "playing her new electric guitar."

"No!" said Lorinda, staring at her friend in horror. "He *didn't*!"

Jenny nodded.

"Why on earth—what reason could he possibly invent for giving that child—*that* child—an electric guitar, beyond the assumed reason of torturing you?"

"Oh, as for the torture, she plays at his apartment too." Jenny sighed. "As for reasons, he told me, quite cheerfully, that she *wanted* one, and of course she mustn't be denied any outlet for her marvelous *creativity*, you see?"

"I see," said Lorinda. "And the ballet lessons you tried to send her to—they had nothing to do with creativity?"

"She didn't like ballet. Found it *confining.*"

"And the piano lessons?"

"The piano was so *obvious*, and so tonally *limiting.*"

"Not to Mozart, but never mind," said Lorinda.

Jenny shook her head. "She's just like her father—she simply will not do what I want her to do."

A series of fairly recognizable chords rained down from above for about ninety seconds.

Lorinda said, "I suppose *he* plays electric guitar?"

"The only thing he plays is the CD player," Jenny said mirthlessly.

Lorinda laughed anyway. "So she's 'self-taught'?"

"Oh, Jimmy's probably helped her. Or Pierce will probably unearth some dirt-ball hippie who used to play rhythm guitar for a third-rate rock band, and get *him* to instruct her in the finer points," said Jenny. "Pierce does take music seriously—or, I should say, as seriously as he's capable of taking anything, which ain't much."

There was a crescendo of elephant sounds for perhaps forty-five seconds, then no more electric guitar music.

"I see she takes it really seriously too," said Lorinda dryly. "Well, what can one expect?"

"One might expect someone more like your Jennifer, mightn't one?"

But Lorinda missed any irony, and said, "Well, people such as Jennifer are in fact *very* rare, the percentages of—"

"Of course, of course," said Jenny. "She's a very, very special child. I was just speaking in a general way, about deportment and so on."

Lorinda put her hand over Jenny's. "I know what you meant. But you cannot forget: You didn't concoct Dolores's DNA all by yourself."

"Meaning I'm forever doomed because she is, what would you say, *infected* with her father's biological imprint?"

"Something like that, I'm afraid. But at least you can figure out how to fight it."

From the staircase off to the side of the living room came Dolores's voice. "And my brother, who is on an academic scholarship to Cornell and is a second-team All-American at ice hockey and has cut four CDs of his own compositions with a jazz octet and is right now working two summer jobs— is *he* infected too? Or is all of his talent just *your* doing?"

"I refuse to respond to people who resort to eavesdropping," snapped Jenny, springing up. "It's as bad as reading someone else's mail."

"Which you *also* did, in Daddy's own *apartment*, when you thought he was falling in love with Jakee," said the voice. "You even looked at his *phone bill*. I *watched* you!"

Lorinda pulled Jenny back down to her seat with some difficulty and poured her the last of the wine. Jenny's eyes were spilling tears, though she was not weeping.

"Have some cheese," Lorinda said lamely.

Jenny shook her head and stared at her plate. After a while, she said, "Oh, God, what can I *do?*"

And Dolores's voice, from farther up the stairway, said, "And if you figure that one out, tell me what I can do too."

Lorinda could not answer either of them.

a multiplicity

IN THE LOCKER ROOM, AS THE HOWELL SCHOOL BOYS are making the transition from their blazers and ties and corduroys to their underwear, William is not especially comfortable with all the undressing. Some guys lounge and strut as if they were catching rays before a game of beach volleyball. Roanoke Wilson is one of these. Today, William cannot help but notice, Roanoke wears green boxer shorts with dollar signs on them.

William wonders: Does the yen to hang out in underpants go along with athletic stardom?

But this unsavory line of thought is cut off, as William hears Roanoke say, "I think at Cathy's party tonight I'll go after that Dolores chick—she's scholarship, and you *know* those poverty-type girls usually want it pretty bad."

This pronouncement evokes knowing laughter and the usual snorts and leers that greet Roanoke's proclamations of sexual intent. But *this* boast is different for William. This one causes William's heart to plummet, like a taut little widgeon who was happily flying along in the sunlight until he felt the deadly push of pellets from somewhere along that nice stretch of lakeshore below. Over and out. Splash. William hustles into his gym shorts and out into the gym to shoot some futile bricks at the basketball hoop.

Dolores! Dolores *is* different. Dolores is on scholarship, everybody knows that, but so was her brother at Howell, and *he* was captain of three varsity teams his senior year and the coolest guy in the school. Dolores herself certainly shows no signs of feeling inferior any more than Jimmy did, and she certainly does whatever she wants in her own way—wears no makeup, plays ice hockey in a travel league with boys (William has snuck into several of her games), wears leather ankle boots with lug soles as school shoes while all the other

St. Elizabeth's girls buy things that make their feet look small and pointy and bright. And on top of it all she is simply more gorgeous than any of them, though in a decidedly stranger way, a way that the others can almost dismiss as being too odd.

During the last party William attended, he found himself on a stairway with her, speaking rather eloquently about music, *his* kind of experimental music, and he knew he was interesting her. *Fascinating* her even, with his long-winded description of improvisation in contemporary art music. William himself plays the members of the clarinet family. Dolores, seemingly unwilling to break contact with him as people walked up and down the stairs between them, kept him locked in with those intense greenish eyes and did not seem to mind in the least that he forgot his manners for many minutes and neglected to allow her a chance to enter the conversation.

Finally he recalled himself, and asked, "And do *you* play an instrument?"

"I fool around on electric guitar," she said, explaining that she mostly copied solos from records. After he assured her that this showed a very good "ear," he pressed her to name some of her favorite tunes, and, seeming suddenly uninterested, she said she had been working for two months on Eric Clapton's solo from "Little Wing" on the 1970 Derek and the Dominos album.

"Wow," William said. "That's an ambitious solo."

Her eyes perked up. "You know it?"

"Yes. It's majestic."

"Well," she said with a half grin, "at least it's *slow*."

Back in gym class it is a pickup hoops day. William finds himself on a team with the braggart Roanoke. Now, in general, because he is taller than anyone, William gets many rebounds, but instead of going right back up for layups (during which his arms are hacked and his kidneys punched), he finds it more interesting to dribble to a spot just short of the foul line, turn with the ball above his head in both hands, and scout for cutting teammates, to whom he threads killer passes so that *they* get layups. Roanoke, a born gunner, understands this all perfectly well and is constantly slipping his man to get open for a William assist. In this game he scores a lot, often shooting a split second after William finds him with a wily pass.

After the game, in the locker room, Roanoke plops down next to William and peels off his sleeveless T-shirt, displaying his perfectly defined abdominal muscles and half-moon pectorals.

"Great looks," he says. Fortunately for William, he knows that in cool-sports parlance, a pass is a "look."

"Thanks," says William, keeping his sweaty shirt on.

"That one time when I went backdoor on Falk, I wasn't sure you were going to see me, but I zipped through the blind spot and *pow!*, there was the ball, and I barely got control of it on the way up for the jumper."

"It *was* a bang-bang play."

"Swished that one," says Roanoke carelessly, as if any other outcome were unthinkable. Meanwhile William has worked his shorts off and is trying to put on his trousers sitting down.

"Hey," says Roanoke, giving him an appraising look, "why don't you drop by Cathy Perry's tonight? Matthews is bringing a mini keg of Sam Adams he got a bum to buy for him yesterday."

William tries to shrug, which throws him off balance in his trouser work. "Sure. Maybe."

"See you there, then," says Roanoke, giving William a poke in the shoulder and moving on into his waiting crew of admirers. The punch knocks William half off the bench and spills all of his change from a pocket.

So as not to seem too eager, William has his dad drop him near the party about an hour after its official starting time, and when he approaches the house, he sees things are already in full swing. The front door is wide open, though it is chilly February. There is extremely loud music puffing out like smoke from a smoldering fire. William imagines these kids who have never heard Xenakis think this stuff is *rough*. He enters. The amenities are not entirely missing: Cathy, his hostess, finds him within two minutes and, though she clearly does not know him, takes his Polarfleece pullover and invites him to have fun.

"There's food in the kitchen and dancing in the dining room, though please don't put any wet drinks down on the wooden table, and I've *tried* to keep the pot smokers outside although I suspect they've crept back into the basement." She waves and makes to move away.

William calls her back. "Excuse me," he says, "but could you tell me if Dolores is here?"

"What *is* it with Dolores?" snaps Cathy. "Roanoke Wilson is already acting like there are no other girls here." She waves a careless hand. "She's somewhere. Look for *him* and you'll find *her*, most likely." Off she struts.

William wends his way through the crowd, saying the obligatory if not especially welcome hello to people he knows from school or other parties, all of whom answer with a belated air of surprise. William is not exactly a party guy, as a rule; he tries to go to the year's first party, which kind of kicks things off in September, and to the last, which closes things down in May; but these February sorts of fetes, which require a certain special effort to attend, are usually far beyond his ken.

Suddenly, up ahead, he spots the back of Roanoke's head. Perhaps Dolores is just beyond.

And for the first time since deciding to come to the party, William thinks of what he might say to her.

Nothing—certainly nothing as an opening gambit—springs to mind. "Hi! Guess what? I still play the clarinet!" hardly possesses the needed conversational punch, and that's about all he has to offer. He can imagine the suave Roanoke looking on, sniggering behind his Boston beer.

Then William remembers: the cassette tape. He did not come *totally* unprepared; in fact, he brought with him a ninety-minute tape concocted of several of his favorite improv pieces, with which he hopes to entice Dolores's ear and interest, if not in him then at least in the music. He pats his pockets but cannot locate the hard plastic case. It would be pretty stupid to stroll up to Dolores and say, "Hi, I made you a tape," without being able to produce the tape itself. Now where did he put it?

His pullover. The one Cathy took away somewhere. He remembers sticking the tape in a zippered pocket of his Polarfleece pullover. Good. Now all he has to do is locate the depository of coats, retrieve the tape, and find Dolores; then he will have something for initiating a conversation.

He looks for the coats in a couple of upstairs bedrooms, but they are dark and people are thrashing on the beds; he closes the doors quickly. He finds Cathy's father's study, but it holds nothing but computer equipment. In the basement he finds a den, but it has indeed been taken over by the pot smokers, the usual red-eyes circling a major blunt, beside a stereo sending out an endless loop of techno riff. *Boom ticky boom.* One smoker, lips pressed tightly to hold in his own smoke, raises his eyebrows at William and extends the blunt, but William shakes his head and leaves.

Back on the first floor, down a dark hallway from the kitchen, he opens a door and finds himself in cold and darkness. His hand locates a switch. He flips it on long enough to see that this is the garage, and in front of him is a fancy Jeep Grand Cherokee that has been heaped with about fifty pieces of outerwear—coats, ski jackets, scarves, parkas, pull-overs like his. The clothing has not completely obscured the windshield, however, and through it, sitting in the driver's seat behind the steering wheel with her arms crossed over her chest, look-ing very cold and cranky, he sees Dolores. She loosens one arm first to motion impatiently at the light, then to motion him to the passenger door. He snaps off the light and finds his way in the dark to the door, which he opens and shuts as quickly as possible, keeping in the heat.

"Close it quietly," she says, which he has already done.

"I see you too are having fun at the party," William says.

"A blast. Some stud from your stupid school has apparently decided to deflower me tonight after filling me with amber beer, and this is the most remote, darkest place I could find to hide from him. I've been here about an hour and a half and had only one bad moment—when Cathy opened the door a few minutes ago to toss in a new coat, but she didn't even turn on the light or look where she was aiming, so I was safe. What are *you* doing here? I know perfectly well you're not the type to run around scouting for this stud."

"I'm looking for my coat. It was probably the one Cathy just tossed in."

"Then you must have been here all of ten minutes, which means you're having a grand old time too. Bad news, by the way—I'm afraid Cath missed the general pile of outerwear and winged your jacket over there by the lawn mowers, where there are likely to be lots of pools of oil and stuff. If I were you I'd— But *were* you leaving?"

"Not quite yet. I was looking for the coat because

I left a cassette tape in the pocket."

"Some party-rock to slip on the stereo for the airheads? You disappoint me. I would have thought you of all people would be above that."

"Oh, I am. Actually, it's not a tape for the party—unless Cathy wanted to clear the house in four or five minutes. It's a tape I made for you. A tape of—well, the kind of music we were discussing earlier in the year. But perhaps you don't remember."

She turns her face and looks at him and her green eyes widen. "Of course I do. It was a terrific talk. I'm sure it's a terrific tape, too. And—it's for *me*?"

He turns and looks at her in the moonlit front seat. She seems unusually moved. "Sure," he says. "For you to—well, you seemed interested, and I put together some pieces from various records, things I thought you'd like—"

"That must have taken hours."

It did. So there in the car all he could do was shrug.

She says, "You know, I bought a few CDs after we talked, stuff you mentioned. But whenever I put one of them on, my mother threw a fit and talked about 'devil headache music,' so I haven't had the chance—"

"You can stick this in your Walkman and she won't be able to hear a thing. As far as she'll know, you'll be listening to good ol' Pantera." He waits for her chuckle to end, then says, "Do you mean to tell me that you bought some CDs just on the strength of talking to *me*?"

"Sure, but don't go wetting your pants over it. It's pretty cool music, what I could hear—very interesting. You're interesting too, as it happens, but the music is the coolest. May I have the tape, please?"

"It's in my jacket," he reminds her. He adds, as if in warning, "Most people find it really difficult."

"Most people find morality difficult," she says, "and chemistry, and the Japanese language, but *they* all work pretty well if you put your mind to it. Thanks a lot for making the tape, wherever it is."

And for half an hour they are off on a talk, about music composers and players, writers, the impossibility of drawing well in art class, the strange appeal of abstract math and the hateful concreteness of algebra, strange fashions in shoes and pants, odd-shaped heads that seem to recur in famous people. As he watches Dolores talk, turned in the seat toward her, William cannot fail to take awed stock of her beauty even in the dim blueness of the light through the garage window—her wide, high cheekbones, the clear eyes that flash instead of move, the thick eyelashes, the slightly cleft chin. At one point she claims she has fallen in love with tenor saxophonist David Murray.

"But not Roanoke Wilson?" he says.

Oops. As soon as he says it, he knows he has goofed, big-time. Dolores's eyes flare. She says, in a voice tight with a tense inquiry from which he knows he cannot escape, "And how did you know *he* is the one I am hiding from tonight?" She stares at him; then suddenly her eyes take on a look of horror. "Oh, God. Don't tell me. He was bragging, doing some sort of premature rooster-on-the-prowl boasting at your school—probably in the *locker room* or something—"

William looks her in the eyes, which is hard, and says nothing, which is also hard. Strangely, now that he has the chance to condemn the other boy, he finds it difficult to do. Roanoke seems so pitiful under the scorn of Dolores.

But he doesn't need to condemn Roanoke. Dolores has the idea. "You're not saying anything because you're trying to maintain that Howell-brotherhood crap. But I *know* he announced that I was just another piece of helpless prey, which he would impale with his mighty saber at *this* particular party." She snorts in exasperation and fixes William with a furious, helpless eye. "But you know what? That dickhead has never even *spoken* to me. He never will, either, because he has the idea he—"

"Excuse me," says William, "but I don't think it extends to the level of 'idea.'"

She stares at him.

"See," William goes on, "Roanoke has great pecs, and clearly defined abdominals, too, and, for that matter, that special arch-eyed expression of tousled naughtiness. What more does he need to be irresistible? Certainly not *ideas*." William smiles. "Roanoke Wilson is still waiting for his first idea."

Dolores watches him for a moment, thinking. Then she nods, and blows air out of puffed cheeks. "My whole life would be a lot simpler," she says, "if I could just be a sucker for clearly defined abdominals." She shakes her head. "It's too bad muscles leave me as cold as this Jeep."

Then she cocks her head at William. "*However,*

she says to the innocent young artist with a coquettish leer on her temptress lips, what *really* turns me on is the mouth of a man who can blow the B-flat clarinet."

And before he can move, she slides across the two feet between them and places a soft, warm kiss on his lips, with her own slightly parted. Then she tucks her head down to his shoulder, and he passes his arm behind her back.

"Don't worry," Dolores says, her voice muffled. "We don't have to get married now."

"What if I want to?" says William.

"Too bad. I'm saving myself for Steve Yzerman."

William says, "I suppose that's a relief. I don't know anything about girls, or women, or whatever you are. I mean, I haven't got the slightest idea how to, you know, attract you or anything."

"Cutting a personalized tape of weird music that sounds like factory noise ain't a bad start," says Dolores, snuggling closer. "But I warn you, it doesn't work for *every* chick."

They sit in their mild hug. It's a lot warmer in the Jeep this way. Twenty minutes later, when Cathy Perry crashes open the door from the house, flips on the light, and begins rummaging in the coats on the hood of the Jeep, this is how she finds them as she looks through the Cherokee windshield. She shrieks and flings herself backward.

Dolores calmly slides over to the driver's window, lowers it, sticks her head out, and says, "Relax, Cathy, it is only I, being peculiar."

"Dolores!" Cathy laughs nervously, flicking a look at William. "Where on *earth* have you been! People—*people*, you get me?—have been asking for you all night!"

"He's yours, Cath, abs and all," says Dolores, opening her door as William opens his, and hopping out. "As you can see, I've been hiding from him in the darkest hole I could find."

Cathy laughs again, nervously, and flicks another look at William. "But not hiding alone, I notice."

"No," says Dolores, turning to give William an appraising look. "This gentleman—it's William, isn't it?—and I have been having a couple of hours of uninhibited sexual intercourse in here on the standard dual airbags. We have in fact just managed to deflate and repack them into their dashboard compartments, which, let me tell you, took *quite* a bit of nifty folding and wedging—"

By this time, under cover of Dolores's badinage, William heads for the fleet of lawn mowers to seek his pullover. He finds it hooked on the handlebars of the only push mower, hovering perilously above a pool of oil. He extracts the tape, holds it up for Dolores to see, then brings it over and hands it to her. She sticks in into a jeans pocket as she talks with Cathy, who is saying, "—so what on *earth* am I supposed to say to him?"

Dolores turns to William. "William. Do you have any good suggestion about what Cathy might say to Roanoke Wilson to console him for the fact that he couldn't locate me all night, a fact for which he, apparently, and rudely, holds her responsible?"

William thinks for a second. "Well, you could tell him he has a killer jump shot inside fifteen feet."

"*There* you go!" Dolores says, patting Cathy on the shoulder and guiding her back toward the door. As soon as the girl is gone, looking slightly dazed, Dolores turns. "Now, William—will you walk me outside to wait for my dad to pick me up?"

She takes his hand without waiting for an

answer and leads him back through the house. As they pass through the kitchen, William catches sight, from the corner of his eye, of a clot of Roanoke's usual crowd, laughing as their hero shotguns a cheap beer upended on his lips. Some of it—quite a bit, actually—trickles down his neck.

"What a guy," says Dolores, pulling William through the crowd.

When they get outside, Dolores says, "Let's go down half a block or so, to get away from the party and the spillover." As they walk, holding hands, she explains that she always asks her father to come for her at least a half hour before a party is scheduled to end, because she usually doesn't have much fun at these things, and also—as they tend to be convened on Friday nights—she often has an ice hockey game to play very early the next morning.

They stop on the sidewalk, a good distance from the noisy house, and stand with their hands in their pockets now.

"Thanks for the music," Dolores says with a smile.

"Thanks for the kiss," says William with a smile of his own. "It's my only one."

"You're sure your mother—?"

"I mean—"

"I know what you mean," she laughs. Then, before he can so much as pull a hand free, she gives him another kiss, quicker and warmer here in the naked night air.

"There." She smiles. "Now at least both of us can say we have accomplished a technical multiplicity of them."

"A multi—both—you mean, *you* never did this before either?"

She pretends to frown, as a set of headlights rounds a corner two blocks away and swings onto the street. "What kind of girl, or woman, or whatever, do you think I am?"

The car stops by them. It's her father, in a very old Volvo. William catches a glimpse of the backseat and sees an enormous canvas bag, a pair of ice skates, and two wooden hockey sticks with ragged tape on the blades. Dolores introduces him to her dad, a small, intense-looking guy who leans across the seat to shake hands enthusiastically. He offers William a ride home anywhere in the city. William, returning the firm shake, declines the ride, saying his own father is on the way to pick him up too.

Dolores slides into the passenger seat as her father goes back to the wheel. She rolls down her window.

"You know what?" she says.

"What?"

"I'd like to hear you play something sometime. You know, in your group. If you have, like, a recital or something."

"Oh," he said. "Yes. Sure. That would be great. Usually not even parents can stand to come and hear us. And—"

"Yes?" she says, both elbows on the window's edge.

"I'd like to come to one of your hockey games, see you skate and all. I don't know much about the—"

"You've already been at three of my hockey games," Dolores says without rancor. She smiles. "I've seen you. A quiet guy with his hands in his pockets kind of stands out among the rabid parents hammering on the glass."

William blushes terribly. "Well. I don't know why I lied just now, but I was embarrassed and—"

"Don't sweat the fib," Dolores says with a half

smile. "We'll just say you were fishing for an *official* invitation."

"What are you doing at five thirty tomorrow morning?" calls her father across the front seat.

"Sleeping, I think," says William.

"Wuss," says her dad, with a smile and a shake of his head.

"Um—why don't I call you?" William says to Dolores.

"Why don't you do it, um, soon?" she says with a smile.

"Yeah," says William, "soon. During wuss hours."

She laughs and begins to roll up the window and the car pulls away. William waits. He watches the direction the Volvo takes, until his own father arrives twenty minutes later.

rah

AT HER PREVIOUS SCHOOL—AN ALL-GIRLS PLACE called St. Elizabeth's—where she had gone for the ninth grade before transferring to the public high school called Central, Dolores had been a cheerleader. Big deal; she had decided to do it by default, after getting cut from the varsity fieldhockey team for playing too rough and being unable to control that little ball with those ludicrously small-bladed sticks, and also for never being able to learn that little perverse business about not twisting your stick in certain situations so you could control the stupid thing better. She would play ice hockey for her travel club in the winter—but she felt like doing *something* in the fall. So cheering for her field-hockey betters and the boys' teams had seemed like a decent idea.

Now, at Central, she read a notice that tryouts for fall cheerleading were coming up, so she decided to give it a whirl once more. However, shortly after arriving at the designated room, she realized that the duties and status of cheerleaders here at Central were not at all what they had been at St. Liz's. There, the cheerleaders had the simple job of whipping up loud enthusiasm from the crowd watching the game—getting people to holler. The better the cheerleaders were, the louder the fans screamed, and the more the athletes on the field felt their support and determination. It was direct, and easy.

But at Central, the privilege of being a cheerleader seemed more to depend on good ol' *cuteness*, and something else, too. Not just impossible peppiness and worse desperation to be a star, such as inspired that famous mom in Texas to hire a killer to murder her daughter's chief rival for a spot on the local squad. No, at Central, cuteness must be complemented by a strange thing generally called *popularity*, though Dolores met few girls who actually liked the girls so designated. The most *popular* girls at Central seemed to be the ones most envied, for their cool boyfriends or their wealth or the social prominence of their families. These were the ones chosen to wear prissy uniforms and perform Central's bizarre brand of "cheerleading": bouncing their tits and tails between the audience and the game to offer a kind of pre-*Playboy* distraction to the audience in badly choreographed little dances set to terrible rhymes meant to connote "support" to the athletes way out on the field.

As a new student unblessed in any of these arts and categories, Dolores knew she was going to have a difficult time meeting the basic qualities needed for eligibility on the cheerleading squad. Nevertheless, when the day came, there she was, determined to try out.

In the audition room, the first three girls performed their little jump-jump squeak-squeak routines before the single judge, last year's captain, a stern girl named Mary with a can of Diet Coke that she never touched at her elbow, holding a pencil with which she never made a note. To Dolores's eye and ear, these girls were uniformly lame as inspirations to make fans root for the hard-fighting players of football, lacrosse, basketball, hockey, or soccer, laboring nobly and muddily on fields beyond; yet the girls were perky and pretty in a magazine–zit-ad kind of way, and they were told immediately that they had made the squad. They acted shocked, though Dolores could tell the only thing that would have *really* shocked them would have been the opposite judgment, and they left giggling and weeping at the same time, a neat trick she would see many times when Central won a game.

The fourth and fifth girls apparently lacked some ineffable something, though to Dolores they seemed slightly louder and more directly cheerish than the previous three; these two were dismissed peremptorily, and they left in tears only. So it went, through six more hopefuls, with two making the grade for no apparent reason related to cheering while four went down in flames without showing any significant difference from those who succeeded.

Dolores went last.

"New girl?" asked Mary in her minimalist way, displaying absolutely no interest; Dolores had detected a mean and iron spirit beneath her falsely charming demand for fealty from the other girls.

"Not really," said Dolores. "I've been one all my life."

This evoked some laughter, which Mary quashed with a glance. She put on a condescending smile. "Pardon me for being unclear. I meant to inquire if you were a new student at Central this season?"

"Yep."

Over murmurs of incredulity from the audience—how could a new student, about whom nothing could be known, try out for cheerleaders, that pinnacle of registered popularity?—Mary said, "May I ask why you want to be a Central cheerleader?"

"You may, even though you didn't ask any of the other candidates. I want to be a Central cheerleader because I like to make people *scream*." She smiled her sweetest, right into Mary's baby blues, then looked over at the couple dozen girls who had come to watch tryouts. They seemed to shrink from her slightly and did not look at all interested in screaming. She returned her smile to Mary. "In this case, of course, to scream for the victory of Central's valiant athletes."

"Yes, of course. All right," said Mary, crossing her arms. She nodded once at the audience, then looked back at Dolores with a flat expression. "Very well. Make us scream."

And Dolores did just that. Yelling at a volume that at first shocked everyone in the room but quickly became rather hot and soulful, pumping or whirling her arm to indicate the imaginary team of bloody gladiators grunting in the mud behind her, and jamming out primitive rhymes and phrases less like the usual chirpy cheers than like the pounding of hip-hop, she whipped the two dozen girls, despite Mary and their loyalty to her, into a hollering, hooting frenzy, without so much as a phony cartwheel or split. She had them jumping up and down, she had them yelling out of sync, a real no-no for cheerleading types but a natural means of expression for the excited human being. It was loud, it was rude, it was undeniably exciting and would be so to any athlete within a hundred yards. Only Mary sat unmoved.

But Mary couldn't fight the frenzy alone. To cheers of congratulation, Dolores was told, rather coolly, that she had taken the final, *optional* open spot on the cheerleading squad, which was now complete.

As they were changing into their cheerleading uniforms before the pep rally on the Friday afternoon before Central's first football game—the unveiling of the new squad—Mary sidled up to Dolores and said, "We have to have a quick chat."

"What about?" asked Dolores as she tugged the thick white sweater down over her not inconsiderable breasts, which were large enough beneath the sweater to make the stiff new red-chenille C on the front stand out like a sandwich board.

Mary eyed this effect with distaste. She had very small breasts, and her well-laundered C curved along them nicely. "About style," she said.

Dolores looked at her. "You mean hairdos and nail polish? Or you mean yelling versus simpering?"

"I would hardly call our choreography 'simpering,'" Mary said frostily, "though 'yelling' sounds about right to describe the dignity of *your* method of leading cheers."

"It's not supposed to be *about* dignity, is it?" asked Dolores, pulling on a saddle shoe. "What the heck is dignified about *football*, when you come right down to it?"

Mary ignored her comments. "I want to make sure we are all—in line, with the same methods of raising pep from the student body today," she said, in what was obviously a speech she had prepared against the odds that Dolores would be difficult.

"Meaning you want me to smile and shake my moneymaker and giggle with the rest of you and do all those queer jumpy 'Gimme-gimme-a-C!' things without raising my voice beyond what I would use to answer a question in French class, or raising the temperature in the room beyond fifty-eight degrees."

"Exactly." At least she was plainspoken, Dolores thought.

"And what about at the game tomorrow?" said Dolores. "This is just a quick little skit in the gym, with the team guys lined up behind us tugging on their tie knots and picking their pimples uneasily as they stand looking more like the Latin Club than a football team. But when we're outside to-morrow and these same guys are smashing each other and spraining their knees and yelling for linebackers to cover running backs in motion in the other team's backfield and no one, *no* one, can hear or give a hoot about you and your cuties to give-you-give-you-a-C!, seems to me some hollering will be *just* what is called for then."

"Well, then we'll deal with that supposed need at that time. Right now, I would like your promise that for this pep rally—"

"No way. If I am a good, polite little quiet thing for the rally, you have to cut me loose to get some *real* cheering going tomorrow. That's the only deal I'll make."

Mary studied her and thought for a moment. "All right," she said, perhaps a little more readily than Dolores was quite happy with. "All right, that can be arranged."

Dolores had neglected to recall that cheerleaders at a football game are placed facing the audience in a long line one every ten yards or so, their configuration entirely determined by the captain. So when Do got to the field the next day, she was told matter-of-factly by Mary that she would be at the end of the line, facing section QQ, way down at the end of the field where a couple of sycamore trees had actually been allowed to encroach on the space surrounding the hallowed gridiron. She would be dead even with an end zone, while Mary stood at the fifty-yard line and her favored cutie pies occupied the primo places on either side of her, facing the vast majority of the crowd watching the game (and, presumably, the cheerleaders' "choreography").

Do stomped down to her outpost, cursing herself for being a forgetful fool. Of course, no fans would be sitting where she was condemned to stand (Mary: "And remember—keeping to our assigned places is very important for general orderliness and the impression that we blanket the whole field with cheer."). If she hollered, it would be at empty cement bleachers. It would even take two relays from Mary down the cutie line to reach her and inform her of what the next "cheer" was supposed to be.

As a last insult, Dolores realized when the teams chose their sides at the coin flip that she would be in front of the end zone attacked by Central during the first and third quarters—so if there happened to be a need for last-minute offensive heroics, they would take place 110 yards due west of her, with the attendant audience and excitement.

The squad, except for the grousing Dolores, practiced a few hoppy cheers called by Mary, while the stands—the ones directly in front of the captain and her cohorts—began to fill up. Only two people joined Dolores in her sycamore-shadowed ghetto: an old bearded man wearing an ancient Central letter jacket the red of which had faded in time to the pink of wintergreen Necco wafers, who was drinking steaming coffee from a thermos; and Dolores's father, who had asked if she would be embarrassed by his presence nearby. Dolores thought the old man in the school coat looked nuts, especially when he pulled a carefully furled pennant from his jacket pocket and unrolled it before sticking it onto the end of a sycamore stick selected for the purpose. He gave the pennant a couple of experimental waves and looked pitiful, Dolores thought.

The game started. As expected, most of the action took place between the forty-yard lines far away. Dolores did not even bother to jounce and handspring for the first few cheers relayed to her, but simply yelped a halfhearted "Go, Central!" instead, whirling a fist. Then something *did* happen in her end zone, but it was in the *second* quarter, under the attack of the bad guys: a Central corner-back fell down while backpedaling to cover the Westlake wideout on a straight sprint pattern down the far sideline, and the quarterback saw it and lofted a bomb, which the Westlake receiver simply had to trot beneath, gather in, and tote across the goal line for an easy touchdown covering seventy yards. The crowd was silent. So was Dolores.

"Young woman!" Dolores heard a crabby voice behind her. She turned and saw the old man waving his pennant madly in her direction. "I say, young woman!"

"Yes, sir?" she said.

"Have you nothing to say when your team is humiliated in such a fashion? Does it not occur to you that *now* is precisely the time when those athletes proudly wearing the colors you yourself are privileged to bear may find themselves in need of some especially well-chosen words of *inspiration*?"

Dolores blushed. "You're exactly right, sir," she said. She snuck a look up the line of the other cheerleaders. Their heads all hung low, and their faces looked as ashamed as if they had just gotten D's in algebra.

Dolores trotted out about five yards onto the field and cupped her hands over her mouth and cut loose with a rusty bellow toward the Central players now slowly lining up for the kickoff.

"They can only score when we fall down!" she screamed. "When we stand tall, they *suck!*"

The heads of a few players turned her way. She clapped her hands in a rough rhythm and kept hollering her impromptu cheer. No little leaps; she stood two-footed in the sycamore leaves and limed grass and screamed until the ball was kicked and returned to about the thirty-five.

She heard a holler from her nearest cheerleader neighbor: "Mary says we are not to freelance, and the use of vulgar language is demeaning and *forbidden!*" Dolores didn't favor her with even a glance.

But behind her she heard the old man say, in a rich, loud baritone, "Now, *that* is more the spirit of the thing!"

For the rest of the half, in which neither team mounted anything like a drive that brought anyone near her end zone, Dolores continued to make up simple slogans—with as many vulgar words as possible, as these tended to get the attention of the players themselves—which insulted

Westlake and lionized Central, and to holler them at the top of her voice. By now, the old man, and her father, too, had learned to wait a couple of seconds and then to match her scream for scream. Once, from the corner of her eye, Do saw Mary put her head down and start to stride down the line to where Dolores was doing her stuff; but apparently the captain thought better of the effort and turned back, leaving Do to her cheerleading fate.

There was no doubt that during the game Dolores and her two fans made more racket than the hundreds of fans in the middle of the bleachers, who were busy watching Mary and Co. spin through cartwheels, and giggle, and cavort, yelling private jokes across the yards between them and laughing all out of proportion, apparently without reference to what was happening on the field. At one point in the third quarter, a bunch of fans actually ran down to Dolores's QQ section to watch the unlikely spectacle of an attempted field goal (high school kickers rarely succeeded) passing through the uprights of the goalpost, to make the score 7–3. Dolores outdid herself improvising cheers on the motif of a kicked ball and other anatomical items of the Westlake team that Central would *also* find its way to kick; she could feel amusement and a certain electric interest pass through some of the people who had run down just to watch the fate of the kick; a few of them even lingered and took seats in QQ, where they stayed to watch the fourth quarter.

They might have momentarily regretted their choice, because with four minutes left in the game, a Central speedster took a punt return and ran it back 56 yards for the go-ahead score (110 yards due west). But by this time even more people had come down to QQ, and Dolores's unexpected ally, the old man with the letter jacket, was facing his mates in the stands and exhorting them to holler with an enthusiasm that matched his own. The color was high in his cheekbones, and between the two of them he and Dolores managed to get their small contingent of rooters on their feet, hollering loudly. She noticed Pierce on his feet, with his fists raised. Beside him, she was surprised to see, was her brother, Jimmy, in the same posture. He grinned and swung one arm in a wave.

Then the worst possible thing for the Central team happened, though it was hardly the worst for Dolores. Perhaps too sure of victory after their late lightning-strike TD, perhaps too tired after fighting from behind for a long day, perhaps drained of adrenaline because holding a late lead is more difficult than catching up and taking one—for whatever reason, the Central defense began to leak. Short passes to running backs across the middle beat straining linebackers a step behind and gained four or five yards whenever needed; a running back who had looked a little slow for three-plus quarters suddenly started turning the corner on sweeps and eating up six or seven yards a pop; a plug of a fullback, whose early runs had been stuffed, now took it up the gut for three yards at a time, usually on third and two. As the clock ticked too slowly, the Westlake offense, like a corps of enemy tanks in a WWII movie, moved inexorably down the field, eating up small chunks of yardage at will and bringing the ball closer and closer to the goal line that seemed to be held only by Dolores and her bearded helper.

The afternoon had worn on, and the light was low and long now; the shadows of the sycamores reached across midfield, which only seemed to further befuddle the Central defense. The slow, relentless nature of the drive allowed the crowd to shift down section by section, until by the last minute of the game they were all crammed into QQ. The pert cheerleaders had moved too but had halted at about the twenty, having run out of pep, or perhaps unwilling to poach on Dolores's turf. Because Dolores, with the game on the line in her patch and the fans standing there in her face teetering on the edge of dejection, was flat on *fire.*

"Stuff the gut stuff the gut stuff the gut!" she screamed, until they picked it up, and the next thing you knew, three of those fullback-up-the-middle runs *had* been stuffed. The athletes were close now, and Dolores could smell their sweat and fear and hatred and cockiness; it was liquor to her. *"Smack the sweep smack the sweep smack the sweep!"* The fans started yelling the phrase, picking up the ferocity at each repetition.

Came the sweep, as if Dolores had been calling the Westlake plays, and, incredibly, it was indeed smacked after the running back had tried an impossible cut upfield and hit a sycamore leaf with his cleats, sliding upright into a big hit from the free safety and landing out of bounds at the ten.

Clock: stopped at 00:04. Down: fourth. Line of scrimmage: officially the eleven. The Westlake players went into a long huddle. And suddenly, as if she were a witch or something, Dolores had a clear vision of what their last play would be. In her mind she saw the line of blockers, including running backs, set up in a half-moon in front of the quarterback, being driven slowly back by the desperate, surging Central rushers; she saw the quarterback floating back, back, back to about the twenty; an unnoticed running back slipping his block and breaking free; and the quarterback lofting a perfect little screen pass over the heads of the outsmarted defense. The back would gather it in. The receivers downfield who flooded the far side of the end zone and drew the cornerbacks and safeties would suddenly turn into surprise blockers and knock the Central defenders on their butts, and the back would high step into the end zone untouched. She saw it in her head, like a newsreel, and she was horrified.

"Bean the screen!" was the best she could come up with as the Westlake players broke their huddle. *"The screen!"* she screamed. Five yards infield from her, in a weary three-point stance, was the huge Central defensive end, a vast black kid named Basil Ellroi. *"Basil!"* Dolores shrieked. *"Bean* it, Basil! *Bean the screen!"*

He looked over at her. Deep inside his bird-cage face mask his eyes had the liveliness of wooden nickels. "Do *what*?" he said, in a voice of unimaginable fatigue.

And then the ball was snapped, and the receivers took off for the far end of the end zone, trailed by Central cornerbacks, and over here the quarterback floated back behind his line of desperate blockers while the Central rushers grunted and dug in their cleats and pushed and strained to get him—

"Bean the screen!" screamed Dolores with a hundred fans.

—and at the key moment a slender speedy-looking kid in a completely clean white uniform bearing the number 20 slipped the line of blockers and looked up to see the ball approaching perfectly over his right shoulder above the frantic, overcommitted Central rush. Calmly, he gathered the ball in, tucked it beneath his right arm, and turned snappily upfield—directly into the cement wall of Basil Ellroi's chest, and the iron wraparound of Basil Ellroi's arms, which picked him up like a thieving cat and flung him contemptuously onto his spotless back still five yards in bounds as the final gun popped at midfield.

Basil Ellroi had listened.

Basil Ellroi had stayed back.

Dolores was close enough to hear Basil in his glory as he faced the wild, shrieking crowd crammed into the small overflowing section of bleachers, and raised both of his arms in the classic biceps-show gesture. He screamed back at them in a voice deep and husky with triumph: *"The screen,"* he yelled, *"has been beaned!"*

Then the players were past Do, making for girlfriends and parents, trying twice and failing to hoist Basil's bulk onto their shoulders as he held his muscleman pose and kept hollering his new mantra. Someone's elbow clipped Dolores, and she spun and went down about as hard as number 20 had.

She stayed down. The autumn earth, churned by cleats, felt good; it smelled good too, among the broken sycamore leaves. And when she finally sat up, her first sight was the back of the old man in the faded letter jacket, rolling up his old pennant as he walked away alone.

fair

LUISA WAS DETERMINED NOT TO SAY IT. BUT JIMMY knew, and he knew she wouldn't be comfortable until she spoke.

He placed his right hand gently on her knee, driving the car with only his left. "Go ahead," he said, watching the road but managing a good look in the direction of her eyes. "Just say it, sweetheart. It will make us *both* feel better. And we have to get it over and done with before we pick up my psychic little sister. Do you want *me* to say it? Because I—"

"No," she said, watching a truck pull out onto Eighth Avenue and cut off a taxi so badly, the taxi had to run two wheels up onto the sidewalk; the taxi kept going about forty anyway. "No," she repeated. "It's a woman's thing to say, and I'm the woman."

He smiled. "No problem with *that.*"

She took a deep breath. "Okay. Here goes. It—it just seems unfair that—it seems unfair for her to get to have a baby before I do. *There,*" she said, with a whoosh of breath. "I said it."

"Yes, you did. But you still feel like crap."

She laughed. *"Sí,"* she said, putting her hand over his. "Maybe just because I want a baby myself. The famous, mysterious compulsion is exhausting. Or maybe it's because I want you and Dolores as my babies to raise." She smiled. "Or Dolores, anyway."

Jimmy laughed softly. "Well, you missed out on *that.*"

"It's probably a beautiful baby." Luisa pointed ahead. "There's the station."

"Okay, right," Jimmy said. He made a quick turn down Thirty-second and within fifty feet saw a car pulling out of a parking place. "A miracle," he said as he stopped and put on his blinker.

Luisa looked at her watch. "A miracle we need.

We'll just be on time for her train. *Maybe.*"

Jimmy swung into the space expertly, ignoring honks from three cars behind him. Over his shoulder he said, "Not to worry. She'll occupy herself by fighting off predators."

They got out of the car. "Must be nice," Luisa said.

"Don't be coy," Jimmy said. "You've fought off more than your share, and you know very well it's not nice at all. But Dolores is pretty tough for being so young."

As they walked, Luisa took Jimmy's hand and smiled. "Oh, I don't know about that. I'd say Dolores is pretty young for being so tough."

"Whatever," said Jimmy. "Maybe both. Here we are." They pushed open heavy doors and walked down a broken escalator.

Penn Station buzzed with people on the move. Businessmen and businesswomen, talking earnestly on tiny cell phones, cutting unseeingly through knots of large families shifting slowly toward gates. Tall, pale boys with rosy cheeks and wispy beards, wavering under stuffed packs on aluminum frames. Beggars slouched against columns, shaking paper cups, being ignored. College students standing in everyone's path, their heads bent with determination over books. And on the fringes of the crowd, men by themselves, following with keen eyes this person or that.

"There she is." Luisa pointed, and Jimmy saw his sister emerge from a stairway, carrying a small backpack by one strap, her thick, wavy hair moving away from her face as she walked. As if Jimmy and Luisa gave off some kind of blips on her radar, Dolores found them with a glance in two seconds. Her only sign of recognition across the room was a quick roll of the eyes.

"Look behind her," said Jimmy with a chuckle.

In Dolores's wake a handsome man of perhaps thirty hurried to keep up with her. He wore a denim shirt with no collar, khakis, and a light sports jacket baggy in the shoulders, with a cell-phone antenna sticking out of a pocket. A very thin laptop case hung from his shoulder; in his left hand he carried a Gladstone reproduction in green canvas and leather and brass. Looking harried but hopeful, mouth chattering, he bumped into people Dolores had just passed smoothly.

"She looks nineteen, and European, and weirdly gorgeous, as always," said Luisa. Dolores walked toward them without a glance in their direction, passing close enough for them to hear the man imploring her.

"—a really excellent cigar bar on West Fifty-third, *great* margaritas, they use only Perfidio—just a drink or two, I can help you find a cab to the place you're staying, or maybe we could get some dim sum—"

Then Dolores doubled back and walked straight up to Jimmy and Luisa, who were both laughing. She hugged Luisa and gave Jimmy a quick kiss. Pointing behind her with a thumb, she said, "I just wanted you to see I wasn't making this guy up."

The man had stopped ten feet away and was watching the three of them with a puzzled look, big wrinkle in his forehead. He said, tentatively, "If you could, you know, use a fourth—"

Jimmy looked at him. "She's my sister and she's sixteen," he said. "'Bye now."

The guy was already gone.

Dolores scowled at Jimmy. "Like it will be okay for bozos to hit on me when I'm eighteen?"

"Welcome to New York," Luisa laughed.

"Where 'haunting beauty' is really *appreciated*," said Jimmy.

"I'll haunt *your* sorry butt."

Luisa said, "Want a doughnut? There's a great—"

"Well, *could* we get something quick to eat? There was nothing on the train but twelve-dollar microwaved pizzas the size of CDs," said Dolores. "Then take me to Brooklyn to ogle this unnecessary sprout of Dad's, and *then* maybe you can take me to a Rangers game or something."

"A seat for the Rangers runs more than your train fare," Jimmy said as they walked out to the street. "Your *round-trip* fare. So maybe after Brooklyn we'll just browse the Barbies at FAO Schwarz or do something else appropriate for a gal your age."

"As long as they have Kens, too," said Dolores. "I've got a thing for really eccentric-looking guys with wild personalities."

Twenty minutes later they were sitting at a sushi bar. As Dolores placed dots of wasabi on a piece of salmon sashimi, Luisa said, "Why 'unnecessary'?"

Dolores held up one hand as, with her chopsticks, she delicately laid a transparent slice of pickled ginger over the rectangle of orange fish.

"Whew," she said, looking at the construction, then at Luisa. Dolores grinned. "I'm always outrageously proud when I can do the ginger with no hands. Unnecessary? Why do I say my father's new kid is unnecessary?"

Luisa nodded.

Dolores looked at Jimmy—he was concentrating on shelling and gobbling boiled soybeans. She said, "You ask because it seems like kind of a cold thing to say about a baby?"

Luisa nodded again.

Dolores dipped the laden piece of salmon in a small dish of shoyu, then ate it. As she chewed, she looked thoughtful. After swallowing, she said, "Well, I can't think of, you know, a graceful way of saying the obvious. Which is, ol' Pierce got to raise James and me, so—what more could he want?" She grinned.

Luisa looked shocked, but she couldn't suppress a laugh.

Dolores kept her grin, went to work on another piece of fish.

Luisa stopped her laugh. She said, "Are—are all babies who aren't as extraordinary as you and James—are they just 'unnecessary' too?"

Dolores, chewing, shook her head and waved her chopsticks. "Not what I said." She gulped her sashimi. "I was talking about my *father*. Not, say, about you and James here. Okay? And besides, I was only joking."

"No," said Luisa. "You weren't joking."

"You're right," said Dolores. "I wasn't."

Jimmy looked at them. "You want some vegetable tempura?" he said, eyebrows up. They shook their heads. He attacked his platter.

"So," Luisa resumed, "that must mean you're actually jealous of little Kim."

Dolores rolled her eyes. "Well, *duh*," she said. "Of course I'm jealous of 'little Kim.'"

"But *why*?" said Luisa. "Because of Pierce? You've had him to yourselves for so long, you're spoiled?"

Dolores pointed with her chopsticks at Luisa's sushi. "Eat something," she said. "At least pick up your chopsticks."

Luisa picked up her chopsticks.

"You say we've 'had him for so long,' right?" said Dolores, dotting a piece of tuna with wasabi and doing it badly. She stopped. "Meaning we should feel we've had him, like, long enough?

Well, you don't have a father for some, I don't know, some *duration* to which you're entitled or something, after which you should give him away to some new kid. You have a father for *life*. He's your father. *My* father. And of course Pierce is Kim's father too now, sure—but I can't help feeling that Jimmy and I had him first. We *claim* him, you know? And a dad like him—well, he's the best, and he's hard to share."

Luisa looked across at Jimmy, in front of whom a crammed sushi board had just been placed. She said, "Have you heard any of this, James? Do you—"

"Do's right," Jimmy said, popping a piece of barbecued eel into his mouth. "I mean, you know, he *is* the best," he said. He swallowed, then grinned, first at Luisa, then at Dolores. "But—hey, *we're* the best too!"

Luisa at last let go with an anger that seemed to surprise both her husband and his sister. "You are both so selfish, you two with your ownership of your wonderful father!" They stared at her. She made a sharp sound of exasperation. Her eyes showed incipient tears. "What about his *wife*?" she said, as if pleading for some vague justice. "What about this, this—*other person*, as you apparently see her? *She* didn't have the great privilege of raising you, the 'best' of children. Maybe she wants to raise a child or two of her own! You never thought of that, did you?"

They blinked. Then Dolores put down her chopsticks, leaned over, and kissed Luisa on the lips. Luisa looked surprised but no less angry.

"You're right," Dolores said. Now there were tears in *her* eyes. "You're right. We're idiots—worse than idiots." She looked at James. He looked at her, then at Luisa.

"Hey," he said, reaching his hand toward his wife. "Hey, I'm sorry. *We're* sorry."

"Tell it to Jin," said Luisa.

"We will," said Dolores.

"But first we'll tell it to you," said Jimmy.

"I don't know why," Luisa said, wiping a tear angrily. "It has nothing to do with me."

"Sure it does," said Dolores. "You want a kid. You're jealous like us."

Luisa gaped at her, mouth open. Then she shut it with a gulping sound, pushed her way out of her chair, and ran across the restaurant, out of the door. Jimmy and Dolores looked at each other briefly, then rushed after her.

When they hit the sidewalk, Jimmy looked to the right, Dolores to the left. Neither saw Luisa. The sun was setting. Jimmy said, "Oh, crap!"

"'Crap'?" said Dolores. "Your wife runs away into the dark of New York, and all you can say is 'Crap'?"

"Not Luisa," said Jimmy, turning back to the door of the sushi bar and reaching into a back pocket. "I didn't pay."

"Gimme," said Dolores, taking his wallet, then pointing. "You run that way. When I come out, I'll run the other way. Whether we find her or not, we meet here in ten minutes."

"Right, okay, good," said Jimmy, taking off. He stopped almost immediately and turned. "Thanks for—"

"Just *go*, will you?"

He turned and ran off.

Dolores went back into the restaurant. Behind the bar, on the other side of all the slabs of lean fish colored pink and white and purple and orange, the main chef ripped off his rising-sun headband and shook a finger at her. "You pay!" he said. "I catch you! You pay now!"

"Oh, yeah, you catch me all right," she said. "Otherwise I wouldn't have walked back in with money when I could be on a subway already." She pulled two twenties from Jimmy's wallet and held them out to him.

Scowling, but less fiercely, he wiped his hands on a towel and took the money, looking at it closely.

"Okay?" Dolores said.

"Too much," he said. "Too much. Wait. I get—"

"Keep it," she said, hurrying for the door.

When she got back to the sidewalk and started off to the left, she realized someone had followed her out of the restaurant. She looked over her shoulder. A thick-haired Japanese man in a gray suit nodded his head in a quick bow as he trotted at her shoulder.

"You need to look for your lady friend who ran away so quickly?" he said, without an accent. Briefly Dolores cussed herself for expecting one.

"Yeah," she said, "but I don't know how upset she was or how far she might—"

"I have a car," he said, reaching into a pocket and lightly pulling her arm with his other hand. "*This* car, in fact," he said, stopping by a black

Lexus. He aimed his keychain at the car; the car issued a beep and Dolores saw the door locks pop up. "We can drive and find her more quickly, cover more blocks." Seeing her hesitate, he said, "This is a crazy area. Crowded sidewalks."

"Okay," Dolores said. She opened the passenger door while he hurried around and popped in beneath the wheel. After he started the smooth engine, the door locks suddenly went down with a *poosht*. Dolores noticed they were the sunken-stick kind you couldn't open from inside.

"Hey," she said.

"Bums try to open the doors when you slow down," he said, pulling out of his space with a *skreet* of tires. "Big delay." The car jumped into the street.

"Can we circle the block in that direction?" she said, pointing. "Maybe my brother has already found her, and we'll see them—"

"Street doesn't go that way," he said, without slackening his speed. In fact, Dolores noticed with alarm, he increased it. The next street bore a one-way arrow pointing the way she wanted to go. But he ran the car past that street too.

"Hey!" she said.

His eyes were on the road. He ran a red light, hand on his horn, and roared to the west, away from sushi and Jimmy and Luisa and what little Dolores knew of New York.

"Whoa, asshole, where—"

He glanced at her with a smile. "You're really beautiful, you know." Eyes back to the road. A taxi screeched out of his way.

"Yeah, so?" She was terrified; she was furious. She let her anger burn her fear. "Is this the only way you can get dates, jerkoff? Besides," she said, embarrassed to use Jimmy's ploy, "I'm sixteen years old. Touch me and it's—"

"Sure, you're sixteen." He laughed. "Those tits, you're sixteen."

"Oh, it's the *tits* you like?" she said. She began pulling up her sweater. "Have a look, then. They jiggle real nice."

He swung his head her way, already starting to gawp. She punched him smack in the nose as hard as she could. His hands flew to the spurting center of his face, hers to the steering wheel. She wrenched it sharply to the right, at the same time pulling herself away from the sudden crunch that buckled the door on her side. The car seemed to lift itself upward in protest, but stopped anyway. An alarm wailed from the Volvo the Lexus had smashed.

The man looked up, grabbed at her hair with one hand. She punched him, this time in the throat. He gagged and scrabbled at his collar, sliding down beneath the wheel. She twisted the keys and yanked them free. The engine died. She pushed a button on the key holder, and the door locks popped up. She scrambled over the man to open the driver's door. Once out, she slammed it.

There was blood on her hands. She looked at it, then pushed the button again. The Lexus chirped, the door locks went down. At least four taxis were honking their horns behind her.

Her instinct was to flip them off, until she realized that her hands were trembling too much even to raise her finger; she also cooled off enough to realize she needed help.

She ran to the driver's window of the nearest cab. The window went down. A scowling dark face, an accented growl, "Lady, what the—"

Through it all, somehow, she had hung on to Jimmy's wallet. She took a large bill from it now and tossed in through the window. The man looked down at it as it fluttered to his lap.

"Can you pull your cab up tight against that car so he can't open the doors on this side and escape?" she said.

"Escape?" the cabdriver said. "Why he would escape?"

"He was going to rape me, okay? So just take that money, pull over, then call a cop."

The driver shrugged and pulled his cab close against the Lexus. Inside, the man, his face looking like a dropped pizza, started to pound on the window. The taxis that had been held up sped through the sudden space, nearly swiping Dolores. This time she did manage to raise a finger at them.

She leaned on the trunk of the yellow cab, hanging her head. She heard sirens in the distance. When she looked up, people were walking by on the sidewalk, staring quickly at her, then at the wrecked car, saying nothing.

She'd thought she would wait for the cops. But as soon as the sirens came closer and closer in the darkening streets, she suddenly threw the keys as far as she could, and ran. When she bumped some-one walking or standing on the sidewalks, she called,

"Excuse me!" back over her shoulder—she noticed her voice was bright and strong. She noticed, with surprise, that she was smiling. She was not someone's sister. She was not someone's child. She was Dolores, and Dolores was the good guys.